Used by the Bratva

Forced Marriage Pregnancy Romance

Morozov Bratva Book 11

Lexi Asher

CONTENTS

CHAPTER 1 - JAMIE

"Isn't life just a blast?"

"Um, what?" I asked, shaking my head as I glanced at the tall red-haired young man seated at the table. "Sorry, PJ, my mind was somewhere else."

The early morning sun brought the perfect temperature to the day. However, it may heat up later, but in the morning breeze, the heat was just enough to keep the chill out of the air.

"Oh, that's okay, Jamie. I was saying that life is a blast, isn't it?" he repeated, rolling his big dark brown eyes at me.

Bringing my cafecito to my lips, I inhaled deeply, allowing the pure flavor of the coffee to fill me with energy. "Yes, it is my friend."

"Where is your mind at, Jamie? Please do share, as you are so obviously distracted by whatever you are thinking of."

Glancing at PJ, he has always been so curious, I can't help but beam. "This latest client of mine, man, the hacking he wanted, required great skill," I whispered as I leaned forward, pushing my breakfast to the side. "But you know it. I got it done."

PJ chuckled as he dragged his chair closer, pushing his plate aside as well. It screeched a little on the white plastic table, but no one seemed to care. "Please tell me more," he insisted trying to force his dense bush of hair in behind his ear.

His hacking skills were admirable, but mine was better. I tried to teach him what I knew, but he was sometimes slow to grasp the entire concept. I knew he would never be able to pull off the type of jobs I did, so teaching him a thing or two was not an issue for me. Placing my cup down and shifting my cap slightly sideways, I leaned in closer.

"Well, you know I don't always talk about my jobs, but this one, this one was a real mind-boggle," I murmured. Before I could divulge more details, my cell rang. PJ glanced at my pocket as it vibrated.

Sitting up straight, I pulled it from my jacket pocket. Glancing at the caller ID before answering. I saw it was Ben, one of my regular clients. I had been doing jobs for him over the last couple of years on and off. He paid me reasonably well and didn't ask too many questions. The fact that he was involved with the Mafia didn't bother me much as I worked anonymously.

"I have to get this," I said to PJ, glaring at me wide-eyed. He only nodded and pulled his plate closer again.

"Hi there," I said enthusiastically. I answered the phone as I rose and walked away from the table. PJ gave me a sideways look, raising his eyebrows as he stuffed sausages into his big mouth.

Covering the receiver of the phone, I whispered to him. "It's private, you know that," I added as I strolled to the curb, glancing back only once to make sure PJ stayed put.

"Yes, yes," Ben replied, sounding rushed. "I don't have time for chit-chat, dear. I have important information to collect."

"Okay, no problem, you know that. Just email me, and I'll get on it right away, as always."

"Thank you, dear, the email has been sent. Talk soon." Ben replied and hung up. He was surely in more of a rush than usual. He has never hung up on me.

Turning back to the table and PJ, I felt a shiver run down my spine, and I shook it off. Ben was always rushed, I told myself as I walked back to the table. Swallowing my coffee, I spoke as I placed the cup down. "Gotta run, friend, talk later."

I took a few quick steps to the curb and hailed a cab. As I got in, I heard PJ calling out. "Wait, what's going on? Your breakfast." His hands were raised as he spoke, and his lush red curls enclosed his innocent face like a wrap.

One day, he would make a handsome man, I thought. At 19, his beard was still only stipples but added texture to his smooth skin. He was tall and skinny, but with age, I was sure he would grow into his baggy clothing. Shaking my head to clear up the strange ideas that suddenly popped in, I turned my attention back to my mission.

Giving the driver my address, I slammed the door shut and waved at PJ as we took off. A little while later, I exited the cab and checked up and down the street out of habit. A hacker never knew when someone would come looking, and I liked to play safe. Nothing seemed out of place or different, so I entered the five-story apartment building where I resided.

The outer façade of red-brown bricks was dirty and cracked; it appeared to be a run-down place. Which, I suppose, it kind of was. Only about ten tenants were still left, and many of the doors and windows in the empty apartments were broken. It wasn't my preferred location, but it was safe for people in my line of work.

I had been saving up half of every job over the last couple of years, and in another year or so, I should have enough to purchase a place of my own. I dreamed of living in the city but couldn't afford it. Walking up to my apartment, I listened for any movement, but the place was quiet. I loved the silence it offered, allowing me to concentrate on my projects.

When I moved to the heart of Miami, I wasn't sure how I would get the same silence, but I intended to find a regular job. I knew my current life was dangerous and didn't want to do this forever. But, until I got something that covered my cost, I would stick to what I knew brought in cash.

Entering my tiny apartment, I ensured the added deadbolts were locked. I couldn't afford anyone walking in on me while I was working. Safety was a significant aspect of staying out of jail and staying alive. I started up my laptop and made coffee while I waited to access my emails.

I read through the encrypted email and smiled. This was going to be a quick payday, I thought. Hacking the site, Ben wanted the information from was a simple one. I sipped my coffee and started toying with the site. I tried several regular entry methods, but it held a couple of blocks.

Not wanting to sit all day, I started a brute force attack before doing an exploit. The system ran for a bit before it allowed me access. As it opened before me, I beamed. "Boom," I said to the screen. Rising, I did my victory dance. I took a couple of turns with my hands in the air, before sitting back down and studying the detail that opened.

Staring at the information, my smile faded along with my good mood. "No, no, no," I mumbled as I put my fingers in my mouth, biting down on them. "This can't be happening." I was always super careful and had never done anything dangerous, or something that could place me in danger.

Seeing the details before me was unbelievable. Ben knew I didn't take on these kinds of projects, and for good reason. I shoved the chair back as I rose in anger. Pacing up and down the small room, I tried to focus my mind. Removing my cap and allowing my short hair to fall out, I tossed the cap at the window.

Bending forward, I pushed my hands into my hair. My mouth opened, but I didn't allow any sound to come out as I screamed from within before taking a deep breath. My insides were all twisted, and it felt like I was about to puke.

Glancing back at the screen, I realized what was done, was done. There was no closing it and not getting in trouble. I quickly sent Ben some of the details he wanted and backtracked my actions. I wasn't going to give him everything I uncovered. I needed some form of security, and the details here would provide.

Grabbing a micro-SD at lighting speed, I made a backup. I could only hope I wasn't in long enough for them to realize or track me. I stuffed the micro card into the small secret clasp of my bra. It would be safe there and on me at all times.

The site contained all the banking details, dealings, hit lists, and more on a couple of extremely dangerous Mafia groups. These included Italian and Russian Mafia organizations. Suddenly feeling like I was baking in an oven, I pulled off the large loose-fitting t-shirt I wore over my crop top and chucked it to the floor.

I paced, biting my nails, and trying to think of a plan. I cleared my prints, but who knew if anyone had traced them or seen me entering? I have never gotten myself in this kind of trouble in my twenty-six years on this planet. I trusted Ben; he knew what I did and didn't do.

How could he ask me something like this?

"No," I spoke out loudly, stamping my foot on the ground. "I'm intelligent. I got this." Sitting back down, I followed my own trail, making sure there was nothing they could track back. After a few hours, I felt sure all traces had been removed.

Taking a deep breath and steadying my heart, racing a hundred miles an hour, I rose and poured another cup. This time, I added some whiskey.

"Yes, I am safe," I said, comforting myself before sending Ben an encrypted message. Without saying much, I simply asked him how he dared ask such a thing from me. I let him know if it came back to me, I would give him up.

I watched the message go through before placing my phone back in my pocket. "Now then," I said to the empty room. "Let's just keep an eye on things for a day or two until we can be sure all is clear."

Leaving my laptop open, I flopped down on the couch in the next room and flipped through the channels on the TV. This was a stupid move. I was sure it was something PJ would have done. I shook my head, still in disbelief, but what could I do now?

TV wasn't something that interested me much, but I left the TV on an oldies show channel. Older movies usually cheered me up when I got round to watching some. My mind was rolling through my actions, and I just couldn't let go. I closed my eyes to ease my nerves and fell asleep at some point.

A while later, waking up, I found night had crept in on me. The moon shone into the room lighting it naturally. Checking my phone, I noticed Ben had not even read my message. Rising, I heard a noise coming from my small old wooden desk in the corner.

As I neared it, I heard the sound coming from my laptop. The laptop was screaming with alarms. This wasn't good. Walking over briskly, I felt my heart sinking to my feet even before I could see what was on the screen as I knew what had happened.

Chapter 2 - Ashan

My meeting was halfway through. I had almost closed the deal with Mr. Urgens when there was a knock at the door. "I'm busy," I shouted, smiling at the man before me. "Apologies for the disturbance," I said to Mr. Urgens.

Since he walked through the double glass doors of my gambling den, he had been on edge. He'd been fidgety and restless even after we entered my office and closed the doors. This deal was important, and I tried to ease him as much as possible. His unrest wasn't quite kosher, and I didn't like it. However, I coped with it, knowing how easily he got offended.

We had a shot of whiskey before we started, and I had thought he looked somewhat calmer. But seeing him jump at the knock on the door gave me a bad feeling. He was about to say something when the door flew open, and Leo Morozov entered.

Mr. Urgens glanced over his shoulder and gave Leo an angry glare. "I am sorry to bother cousin, but something serious has come up that can't wait," Leo said, stepping up to my side.

Leaning in, Leo whispered. Yet, his voice seemed to billow through the air. "Our information base has been hacked, and the details for this establishment were included in the information they got. They got everyone's details. I need to access your network to do a trace."

I tried to give Mr. Urgens a comforting smile but I felt sure my face spoke of the anger rising inside. I felt my blood turning to fire as Leo spoke. Looking up into his eyes, I knew this wasn't a joke. He appeared way too calm for this to be a lie and even though his face was straight, his eyes spoke volumes.

Mr. Urgens rose from his chair quickly, almost toppling it over. "You've been hacked?" He spat at me.

Standing and meeting his gaze, I tried to calm him down. "No, no, Mr. Urgens. Please sit while I go out for a second to find out what is happening. Please."

He was already halfway across the floor as I spoke. Grabbing the door, Mr. Urgens turned; his eyes were lit as if on fire. "I can't have part of such things. The deal is off. I must go." He sputtered, rambling off his words before disappearing through the door.

Feeling my anger taking over, I slammed my fists onto the table. "No," I screamed. I have been working on this deal for more than six months. Working with the Castoia Mafia would have doubled our income. I couldn't believe he had just walked out. Even more, I was stunned at the information Leo had just shared.

Glancing at Leo, I moved away from my desk so he could access my laptop. "What the hell happened?" I asked as I stared out the second-floor window. I saw Mr. Urgens rush to his limo. "There went our relations with the Castoias," I added, irritated.

"Yeah, the timing of this hack was terrible," Leo remarked from behind me. I could hear some stress in his voice. "I'm not sure if they had something to do with it, though." He added.

"Do you think this was planned, and they had something to do with it? Can you trace the hacker?" I asked hastily. After Luder went full-time into real estate, I became head of gambling. He has his own life now with his family, and I have made a real difference in our operations. Yet, today's canceled deal was a blow to us.

"It's not only us; it may have had something to do with the meet, but we don't know anything for sure. I'll let you know once, I'm sure." Leo breathed out as he rose and moved to the door. "I'll be back later, Ashan." he added, slamming the door shut behind him as he left. I glanced at the door in amazement and back out the window.

I didn't expect Leo's action. I sighed, turning back, and staring at the city outside. Opening the window, I allowed the breeze to blow in and cool the sweat forming on my brow. "This deal is my failure," I spoke to the wind. "No matter what happened, it was on me."

Hearing the door softly opening behind me, I spun around to see who was now coming to bother me further. Leaning against the door in her silky gown stood Ana. We had an on and off fling for a couple years now. I even made her part of the management at the den. But the family didn't agree with our relationship. They felt she was slightly vindictive and a bad influence. Yet, I couldn't really see it. Maybe my feelings were clouding my judgment.

I had broken up with her a couple of times, but she had something, I just couldn't place it. She had a lure. The gown she wore wasn't tied and hung to the sides of her curvaceous body. Her lacy underwear didn't leave a lot for the imagination as she stretched her arm up the door. Ana licked her fully round lips and smiled seductively at me.

"Not now, Ana," I said as she entered and closed the door behind her. Yet, she didn't seem the least bit put off by my words or tone.

Walking toward me, she moved her head from side to side so hard that her silky red locks flowed into her face. Ana pushed herself onto my table. Sitting on the corner, she placed her hands between her legs as she leaned forward. "Come on, sweetie," she whispered, pushing her breasts out and shaking them lightly. "I know you want some."

"Ana," I said, raising my voice slightly. "I said not now." My mind was overflowing with the events of earlier. I had to do something to rectify the deal. But first, I needed to find out more about this hacker.

As I stepped past Ana, she grabbed hold of my hand and placed it between her breasts. "Come on, baby, you know it's good. It will help you relax. It always does."

Pulling my hand from hers, I shook my head and left my office. This was not the time for such things. She aggravated me with her constant come-ons lately. We had a good time, but it was short-term. Yet, she appeared not to grasp this. I took what I wanted and didn't want to be tied down. Ana knew this; I had never stayed with a woman for over six months. She had been my longest relationship if you could call it that.

But now I had to make sure that Mr. Urgens didn't talk about what had gone down here. Plus, I needed to know if he had anything to do with this leak. We couldn't afford to have our business splattered around.

Leo's office was empty. He must have gone to Roman, and I would catch up in a bit once Mr. Urgens was dealt with. Leaving the club, I made a couple of calls. I would make sure that business would be taken care of before anything could get out. I wasn't going to let this interfere with our dealings.

Driving towards the Castoia's gambling house, I received a text from my top man. They had managed to get Mr. Urgens before he got to the casino, and he was waiting for me at the warehouse. Changing course, I sped up so I could get back before anyone came looking.

Riding around a two-block area, I ensured no sign of anyone else lurking around before parking next to the warehouse. Upon entering, I found four of my men inside with Mr. Urgens tied to a chair and gagged. They had placed him in the middle of the room.

"Hi there," I spoke to Mr. Urgens as I neared him. "I'm so sorry for the inconvenience. But I am sure you also know I can't allow the news to surface." Grinning at him, I added. "Did you have anything to do with this?"

Mr. Urgens shook his head violently from side to side, mumbling through the gag.

"You know this is only business, no hard feelings. Right?"

He shook his head in acknowledgment and mumbled again. "Right then, you should also know what is coming next," I added, glancing at the men around me. Mr. Urgens started squirming in the chair, moving fiercely. "Now, now, if you do that, the chair might fall over, and you could get hurt. So just sit still for us, and I'll make it quick, I promise."

This older man before me had been in this business a long time. I felt sure that retirement was due. I couldn't be sure if he knew more about the hack, but I couldn't take any chances. I had no other option than to take him out of play. Pulling my Smith & Wesson, I leaned closer. "I am truly sorry," I whispered into his ear.

Stepping back two paces, I aimed for his head. Mr. Urgens appeared to turn white as his blood drained from his face and sweat formed on his forehead. His mumbling increased, but he closed his eyes as I squeezed the trigger.

The shot echoed through the warehouse as blood splattered the floor behind the chair. It was done, but now we needed to get rid of the evidence.

I turned to my main man as I spoke. "Have you brought the barrels I asked for from Roman's keep?" He nodded and pointed to the far side of the warehouse. "Right," I continued. "You know what to do.

"Right away, boss," he replied before showing the others to get a move on.

"No one is to ever speak of this, understood. Once you are done and sure the place is clean, take the drums out on the yacht to the cargo ship just off the port. They will know what to do with them." I said as I walked to the door. The men scurried around, doing as they were told.

With that done, I could focus on the problem at hand: the hacker. I felt sure that Leo had found the invader by now as I headed to his place. Arriving at Leo's, I saw a string of cars lined up outside. The family had gathered to sort out this mess, I thought as I walked in.

The women were all in the kitchen having tea, coffee, or juice while preparing food for lunch. Waving as I passed, I headed upstairs to Leo's den. Entering, I noticed not everyone was present. Sergei was there, but Roman wasn't. Then there was Ivan, Evelina, Luder, Leo, and me.

"Close the door behind you," Leo said as I stepped inside.

"Have you found anything?" I replied as I closed the door and took a seat.

Evelina turned to me as she spoke. "We are still back tracing the hacker's steps. It appears someone else has found our hacker though. But Ashan…" she fell quiet and glanced at Ivan.

"We were lucky. More details than expected were taken from some of the others, and it's been leaked," Ivan added.

Leaning forward to see Ivan clearly past Evelina, I asked just to be sure I heard right. "It's been leaked. What do you mean?"

Leo glanced back at me from his place before the computer. "Our location of the den house is on the web for all to see, Ashan. But we will get to the bottom of it and do a cleanup."

Feeling the blood draining from my face, I placed my head between my hands and took a couple of deep breaths. This wasn't good; once information got out there, it was practically impossible to remove it. "How can I help?" I asked, rising.

"Well," Leo said over his screen. "Once we have more, we will send out some men to check if the information is valid. You focus on rectifying the deal, and we'll keep you updated."

"Okay, already on it. See you later," I said, heading out the door. I felt sick knowing there was nothing I could do to fix this. Even though it wasn't my doing, we could all be in danger. This made my anger spike even more. The family had to be protected at any cost.

I took the backroads, heading back to my gambling den to make some calls. Parking in my usual spot, I sat for a bit, observing. I had worked hard the last couple of years to get this place up and running and now this.

I wasn't sure how much time I would have to clear the place out or get someone to take it out of my hands. I sat and admired my handy work a bit. The place was a wreck when the family bought it. Now, it was one of the most popular gambling dens in the area.

At night, the lights fitted into the dome above lit up the entire area. It is a marvelous creation, even if I have to say so myself. Abandoning it would be a shame. There are three floors of entertainment. At the bottom, the entire place was fitted with the latest gambling machines, a food court, and a dance floor. The second floor consisted of the biggest variety of tables available in Miami and the top. Well, the top is the most impressive.

It included a five-star restaurant, pool area, topless bar, private dance rooms, and so much more. I felt my anger being replaced by a deep sorrow. Stepping out of my car, I slammed the door with force. "If I get my hands on the person responsible, I swear…" I spoke to the building before trailing off as my guards came over.

"Sir," the tall, skinny one said as they came to stand before me. "There's a call for you. It's someone about the deal."

Shoving past them, I entered the building quickly. As I moved to the stairs, I showed the lady at the desk to transfer the call to my office. When I entered my glass office on the second floor, the phone started ringing.

Taking a deep breath, I answered. "Ashan here; how can I assist." I wasn't prepared for the voice blaring back at me over the phone, and for a second, I held the handset out before me, staring at it.

"Ashan, Ashan, are you there?" It was the firstborn son of Mr. Castoia himself, Bonno. I had not expected him or anyone in the family to call. I would have thought they would have had one of their men, do it? But seems I was mistaken.

"Hi, Bonno; what can I do for you?" I inquired, keeping my tone as level as possible.

15

"Is Mr. Urgens still there?" he asked.

"Why, no, he left a couple of hours back," I replied, rubbing my forehead. It felt like the start of a migraine. Sitting down, I pulled my meds from the top drawer and swallowed two pills.

"He is missing; we can't find him, his car, his phone, or anything else. What was his state of mind when he left you?" Bonno continued.

Clearing my throat, I answered shortly, not wanting him to hear the irritation in my voice. "He seemed fine. He said he would get back to me on the details of the deal and left. Sorry, Bonno, but I have to go. Let me know if we can assist with anything else, okay?"

"Yes, okay, fine, thanks." The reply came before the line went dead.

Chapter 3 - Jamie

Staring at the screen, my mind whirled at the speed of light. Before my eyes, was a message; it wasn't something any hacker ever wanted to see. It read, *'Found you, prepare for war!'*

I was still trying to absorb the details when my screen changed, and my personal information flooded the internet. I stepped forward, sat down, and started slamming at the keys, moving from one site to the next, trying my best to stop it. I've been hacked, and my firewalls cracked.

After a couple of seconds, I realized I wasn't going to be able to stop or remove all of it. I watched in horror as my name, telephone number, address, and more leaked out into the open. "No," I screamed at the laptop, picked it up, and chucked it at the wall. Rising from my chair, I knew there would be company coming soon. I grabbed a bag and started collecting the most vital items.

Running was my only option now. I would have to find a place to hide. Ben did this to me, I thought as I pulled my shirt back on and added a hoodie for extra cover. Pulling my phone from my pocket, I stared at the screen. Feeling sure my security on the phone was good enough, I decided to keep it. I kept some of the information I discovered. With this came the realization that the Mafia groups would be looking for me and those who wanted to get to them.

Standing at my door, I wondered where I would go as I put on my coat. I dialed my last client. It was the only number I had for Ben. He has to assist me; after all, it's his fault. "Ben, Ben, you must help. I got traced doing what you wanted. I need a place to lay low." I breathed into the phone as he answered.

"You do know you were paid, and it's not my problem if you get sloppy and are caught in the act." He responded abruptly.

"Really, Ben? You know, I don't do sites where there are traps. You led me there. Now you have to help me." I replied angrily.

"Slow down, let me think for a second," Ben replied in his usual quick manner. "Okay, okay, I have it," he added. "Hang up and get to the address I am sending you now. You can tell them I sent you."

Feeling a tinge of relief moving up my spine, I darted out and headed to the address on my phone. It was still dark out, but morning would come soon. I stuck to the buildings and bushes on the sidewalks as I moved, checking for anyone suspicious. After a while, my muscles burned, but slowing wasn't in the cards.

I wasn't even sure if I'd make it as the address was on the other side of town. Staying low and out of any area with cameras made for slow progress.

By lunch time I was only about halfway. Counting what cash, I had on me left me with very few options. I bought a pack of chips and a water at a corner shop.

Hiding in a brush, I rested my body and appreciated the little food. Looking at the sun's movement, I knew I would be spending the night outside. Getting up, I proceeded with the hope that I would at least get closer to my end destination before complete darkness.

As night finally set in, I estimated I was about twenty to thirty blocks away. I found a secluded spot in an alley hiding behind some dumpsters and settled in for the night. It had been ages since I had slept outside in fear for my life. It brought back a lot of memories I had long forgotten, and my sleep was filled with demons.

Waking in the early hours, I started moving again. I felt sure that I would reach my destination before lunch, hoping that Ben hadn't betrayed me a second time.

Nearing the location, I slowed down to survey the area. I felt my heart pushing up my throat. Between me and the entrance stood a couple of thugs. I thought they had to be from one or the other Mafia group. They weren't beggars or street people. Their clothing was rugged but too neat, and something about their posture just screamed at me.

I didn't know them and couldn't be sure if they could be living in the area, but I wasn't going to take any chances. The buildings in this area were mostly rundown, doors and windows were smashed, there were no gardens and most of the houses looked deserted. This wasn't the type of place I would visit or be caught in under normal circumstances. But the events forced my hand.

Pulling my hoodie further down over my face, I walked briskly hoping to pass them without an issue. As I started to pass , one guy tapped the other on the chest. "That's her, let's go."

I started running as dread snuck in and turned the blood in my veins to ice. Glancing back as I ran across the street, I saw them gaining on me. I wouldn't be able to enter the house as they would surely follow. Who knew what would happen then?

Glancing over my shoulder as I turned away from the entrance to the property before me, my foot caught on the curb, and I went sprawling forward.

Putting out my hands, I managed to save my head from colliding with the stone curb. I slid forward, taking off the outer layer of skin from my palms. Coming to a stop, I knew there was no time to fuss about my bleeding hands. My clothing also looked atrocious now, dirty and ripped. I would now fit in, I thought, glancing down.

Jumping to my feet, I felt pain shooting through my left leg. I thought to myself, this, too, would have to wait as I took off again. After taking a step or two, I started hobbling along as the throbbing in my leg increased. Glancing back again, I felt the blood drain from my body as the two men were on my heels.

The one had pulled a gun and was trying to aim it at me. This came from trusting strangers, I thought as my heart tried to smash through my ribs. Heaving as I moved, I knew this day wouldn't end well. My lungs burned almost as much as my leg, I was battling to breathe, and my head felt light.

The chase hadn't progressed far when a gunshot vibrated through the air. I froze and lifted my hands slowly. Turning, I saw an elderly man standing on the curb by the house I was heading to. He screamed something at the two thugs and started shooting at them.

Noticing they were now running in the opposite direction, I collapsed to the ground heaving heavily. Thankful for the interruption but still shaking from fear I sat in a heap. I wasn't sure if I should go to this place Ben had sent me and if it was safe. The man walked over to me and stopped a couple of feet away.

"You're the hacker?" the man inquired in a low, deep tone. His graying beard seemed to be one with the little hair he had left on his head as it appeared to surround his face. He wore a large dark brown overcoat and brown slacks. Even though his clothing seemed worn, his black pointy shoes shined and looked brand new.

Shaking my head, he waved for me to follow. Dusting myself off as I rose, I reluctantly contemplated my chances on the street.

"Sorry, sir," I called after the man as he entered the property, heading for the door. He stopped and turned to me. "Do you know who those men were and where I can find Ben?" I questioned.

"Yes, yes," he replied, glancing over his shoulder. "Come inside. It's not safe out here."

Scanning the area around us, the street appeared quiet. Those two men were surely Bratva, and they may come back. Entering the yard, I moved little by little as I couldn't shake this feeling of impending doom. The man walked ahead of me as we entered the rundown house.

There was a long hallway with stairs to the right leading up and two entranceways on the left of the passage before us. We moved down it to the open room ahead. The room appeared to be a kitchen with broken cupboards, shelves, and a small island in the middle. There were three people seated around the island.

"Come, come, have a seat." The man said, pointing to the island as he moved around it. My heart was racing, and I felt a slight tremor run through my body. Something was off, but I couldn't place the feelings.

Moving forward at a snail's pace, I kept my eyes fixed on the seated inhabitants. As I closed in on the island, I noticed the one pulling out a knife and lowering it to his side. To my right was what I hoped was a backdoor and a way out should I need to run.

"Where's Ben?" I asked abruptly as I came to stand on the side of the island. It seemed that the three seated were one female and two men. The woman sat on the stool closest to me. Their clothing looked worse than mine, and I noticed their hands and faces were dirty. They made me think of street kids, beggars, and thieves.

I was out of place here; I may be a hacker, but I was nothing like these people. I never associated with people who would stab you in the back for a penny, and that is what I thought of them.

Turning her head toward me, the woman who was younger than me whispered in an airy voice. "He's not coming, love. You are the target." Her words had barely filled the air when the two men slid off their seats.

Knowing trouble when I was faced with it, I turned on my heels and pushed out through the door. Stumbling onto a broken porch, I almost fell over the lifted floorboards. Managing to stay upright, I headed for the back fence. It was in ruin, and there were only a couple of places where it still stood.

"Come back, young lady," the man called after me. "Ben said you need to face the music."

Glancing back as I wiggled through the pieces of fencing, I saw the other three pursuing me. As I stepped through, I screamed back at him. "You tell Ben this is his doing, and he will pay!"

Clutching my backpack, I picked up some stones and threw them at the first one, trying to follow me through the fence. As he ducked back in, I turned and ran. I didn't look back and ran sideways, up, and down streets, through yards and buildings until my legs burnt and I couldn't breathe anymore.

My leg, my head, and my heart were pounding. I felt the excruciating pain as the adrenaline started to wear off.

Cowering behind some dump bins, I pull out my phone. With no other options, I made a call to Pedro. I didn't know him well; he worked for shady people, but if anyone could help, it would be him. We had a one-night stand last year, but he wasn't the kind of man I usually hung around with. Yet, we kept in touch now and then.

I listened as it rang, my heart beating in my ears as I took a couple of deep breaths. "Pedro," I heaved out as the ringing stopped.

"Hey there, sunshine," his voice echoed through the speaker. "How are you doing, I heard you got some trouble, is that true? How can I help?"

"Yes, Pedro, I need help, please."

"I heard through the grapevine you gotten yourself into a sticky mess." He replied.

"Please, this wasn't my doing, I need a place to lay low," I asked quietly.

"Mmm…"

"Pedro, what does that mean?" He was my last hope; if he couldn't help, I didn't know where I would go.

"Well," he replied, sounding excited. "I can assist on one condition."

"Please, Pedro, please, anything, you have to help me," I begged, disgusted at the hint of desperation in my voice.

"Okay, okay, but you have to give me another shot, just one more time with you in exchange for safety, dol," the lust dripped from his voice and made me shiver.

I couldn't believe my ears; did he really expect me to sleep with him again? I sat contemplating the situation, and my fate. He wasn't that bad, but I didn't like people who thought the world revolved around them.

"You still there dol? This is a limited offer, you know," Pedro spat through the phone.

Glancing around, I knew there was no other option. "Yes," I said reluctantly.

"Sorry, can you repeat that? I didn't hear you clearly?" Pedro retorted.

Pulling my face into a scrunch as my heart sunk to my feet, I replied louder. "Yes, Pedro, I said yes, now please help me."

Chuckling, he asked me where I was and then gave me directions to an address.

"When you get there, ask for the boss. Tell him I sent you, and he will assist you. You got that?"

"Yes, yes," I replied quickly and hung up. If I didn't move soon, someone would surely come upon me here. The day was moving along quicker than I had anticipated, and soon, it would be night again. I didn't want to be outside another night.

Staying low and as covered as possible, I moved a bit slower, heading to the location Pedro gave me. After going about eight or so blocks, I noticed I was no longer in the same territory. Ducking behind some bushes on the corner, I surveyed the area.

I knew I was still in Miami, but I felt sure I had just entered the territory of the most feared Bratva in all the states. Moving inward as directed, I saw the cars parked outside this club. There was no more doubt. I now knew that I had entered their territory.

Moving in behind an old coffee shop, I sat for a while contemplating my life. Was the danger this area held worth the risk? What if Pedro lied like Ben? I felt tears running softly down my cheeks and rubbed ferociously at them. This wasn't the time to turn soft, I scolded myself quietly. I couldn't even be sure which information Ben leaked and who it belonged to.

Looking down at my hands, I noticed they were covered in dust, sand, and filth. I could only imagine the lines they had left on my face after rubbing my cheeks and eyes. My heart was beating in my throat, and my legs felt numb from all the running. I couldn't look for another place, I knew I had to trust that Pedro actually wanted me, and he wasn't lying.

Maybe I could find safety here or not, but running was over. I needed rest and could only hope they weren't looking for me or knew who I was.

"To hell with it," I said out loud, moving out from the dark corner. I waited for the traffic to decrease before moving over the street and heading to the address he had given. It wasn't far now, only about three or four blocks. I felt sure of it. I could see no immediate danger, and most people just scurried past me without even a look.

Rounding the corner two blocks up, I saw the big neon sign just up the street. Almost there, I told myself as I lowered the hoodie further and focused on the pavement. My legs felt like lead and appeared to get heavier as I got closer to the gambling den.

I had no other hope, the situation Ben had gotten me into was life or death. I chose life, so I would just walk in and ask for the boss as directed. Stepping up to the door, the valet gave me a strange look. I was sure he was wondering what someone so dirty was doing here.

Ignoring him, I walked through the large double glass doors. Inside, I was met with more disgusting stares, and two guards quickly came over.

"Can we help you with something? Are you lost?" One of them asked as they stepped in front of me.

Glancing up, I saw the guns at their sides. Both were quite large men with short hair, black suits, and no facial hair. They looked more like they could have been clients if not for the weapons. I didn't know what the mafia looked like, but these men surely weren't thugs.

Straightening out, I spoke up. "I'm looking for the boss." I hoped my voice was calm enough to sound professional and didn't portray the fear I felt bouncing through me.

"May we ask who's wanting to see him?" the other guard inquired, sounding less threatening than the first.

"You can tell him Pedro sent me, please," I replied feeling a bit more confident. At least they didn't throw me out or shoot me.

Chapter 4 - Ashan

Leo had told me that someone had come to Roman's place, claiming to have seen the person responsible. He had sent two men to check it out. Now, we waited patiently to hear back from them.

I was staring out my office window when I heard the knock at the door. Swallowing the whiskey I had just sipped, I answered. "Yes?" I expected Leo or one of his men to have news on the hacker.

The door cracked open halfway as I turned around. It was one of my guards popping their head inside. "Boss," he said.

"Yes, man, spit it out." I didn't have time for house problems right now. We had enough other things to focus on.

"There is a woman here looking for you."

"Do they have an appointment? I didn't know I had a meeting." I asked, rising from my desk, and placing my glass down. It was surely Ana returning to try again. Not that I knew why she would send a guard to collect me in such a way. I didn't know if she understood anymore, but I was ready to send her packing if it was.

"She said Pedro sent her, sir," he added, glancing at the floor. "Should we ask her to leave?"

"Pedro sent her?" I said, half confused. Why would Pedro send Ana or anyone else here, for that matter? It couldn't be Ana as I felt sure, I had seen her fighting with some of the cleaners earlier. "No, I'm coming to have a look," I added as I walked towards him, and the door. I was suddenly fascinated to find out who was looking for me.

I followed the guard down to the entrance, where one of the other men was waiting. Before him sat someone at the corner table in the dark. Stepping closer so I could see more clearly, I was astounded. It wasn't Ana as I had concluded. She was surely around quacking at someone somewhere in the den.

What was this? The woman waiting there was messy and covered in dirt. For the life of me, I couldn't understand why Pedro would send such a person here.

Her appearance spoke of living on the street but by her clothes and bag, I felt sure she wasn't or rather hadn't been living on the street. Feeling my anger pushing back up, I spoke hastily in a tone less than soothing. "Yes, how can I help, miss?"

Something in her eyes caught my attention as she glanced up at me. There was something wild in them. She intrigued me even though her face was streaked, and her brown hair was a mess under the cap she wore. The loose-fitting shirt was dirtier than her smooth face, and I felt a pull to her for some reason.

"Please, sir," she said softly. "I will work for you in exchange for protection. Please don't send me away."

She looked a mess, but something inside me told me that this woman before me, even in her state, could benefit me. I couldn't shake the feeling that I needed to help her. I didn't even know why she needed protection, but there was a strong pull.

Yet, after my brother Luder fell irrationally in love so easily, I became a bit cautious regarding women. I shook my head, trying to clear my mind. Why was this dirty woman fogging up my brain? But maybe I could give her a chance and see what she could bring to the table business-wise and not in any other capacity.

"Okay, miss," I said, turning sideways. "Come with me, and we can have a chat."

She beamed as she came closer, ready to follow me. Walking to the bottom office, I entered and told her to take a seat so long. This office was more like an interrogation room, holding only the bare minimum needed. I wasn't comfortable taking her to my office yet. I first wanted to know more.

There was a small table with nothing on, two chairs, and a basin in the corner. The shelves were bare, and the single cupboard held some chemicals, medical supplies, rope, and a bucket. As I left to order some coffee, I noticed her taking off her jacket and placing it on the chair before sitting down.

This was an odd gesture, but maybe she wanted to keep the chair clean somehow. The guards were now both standing just outside the door, so I asked one to get us two cups and a pot of coffee. Re-entering, I closed the door and sat down behind the desk.

She pushed the hoodie back from her head and removed her cap, revealing the hidden beauty. I was entranced and couldn't pull my eyes away. Her brown hair perfectly framed her dirty face, giving it an almost angelic look. Cleaned up, I felt sure she could attract a lot of attention.

Clearing my throat, I spoke up. "So, miss…, sorry, I didn't catch your name?"

She glanced at me with her piercing blue eyes and answered in a barely audible voice. "Jamie."

Raising my voice slightly, feeling irritated, I asked again. "Sorry, your name? Please speak up so I can hear you."

This time, she looked me in the eyes as she spoke. "I said, my name is Jamie, and you are?"

I liked the spark I saw flaming in her as she answered the second time. She was a livewire, which intrigued me more. "Well, Jamie, I am Ashan, you said Pedro sent you. So, what can I do for you?"

Jamie jumped in her seat as the door opened behind her. She looked back with such speed that her hair covered her face for a second. The guard entered and placed the tray with coffee and cups on the table. "Will there be anything else?" he asked, looking at Jamie.

"No, thank you," I responded, waving for him to leave. I poured us each a cup and handed her one. She was very shaken, and I wondered what had happened to send her to my door. "You were saying?" I asked, leaning back in my chair, inhaling the delicious aroma of the coffee.

She sipped from the cup, her lips forming a soft circle before looking at me again. "Pedro told me I could come here, as I mentioned before. I need a place to…," she glanced away as her words disappeared.

After a second or two, she looked back and continued. "A place to stay. In exchange, I could work for you."

Grinning at her, I rubbed my cheek as I considered. "What exactly do you do? What kind of service can you offer? We don't really have a staff shortage at the moment." I was intrigued and raised my eyebrows as I spoke, knowing the kind of company Pedro kept.

Jamie shifted and glanced around the room as if seeking a way out. "Well, I'm pretty good at working on computers. But can pretty much do anything or at least try." She now appeared calmer as she spoke.

"I don't know if we have an opening, though. But tell me more about your computer abilities." I asked. The fact that Pedro had sent her made me wonder.

Jamie slowly raised her cup. She looked at me as she sipped. She no longer looked even slightly jittery or scared. Something changed in her.

Sitting back, she spoke with confidence. "I can basically do anything you want. You name it, and I will get it done." she proclaimed.

Grinning, I wondered what Leo would think. "So, you can do searches to collect information and do such things?" I asked curiously.

"Yeah, sure," she replied, a bit too quickly for my comfort.

"Oh really," I remarked, leaning forward, wondering if she had something to do with the recent hack. I was sure she knew what I was thinking as she protested even before I asked.

"I don't go snooping or do illegal things, though. I only access public details and such." I noticed she was fumbling with the edges of her hoodie as she spoke.

"You seem nervous suddenly," I said, folding my arms. "Is there something I should know? Like the real reason for you coming here?"

"No, no," she responded quickly. "I'm not into anything dangerous or such. Like I said, I'm only looking for a safe place." As the words left her mouth, she realized what she had said.

Her hands flew up to her mouth. She shifted forward to the edge of the chair. With wide eyes, she leaned forward as she spoke. "That didn't come out right. Please let me explain."

I knew she was hiding something. "Now, now," I said. "Calm down and tell me the truth."

As she started, it dawned on me that she could be the hacker everyone was searching for. "Okay," she said, glancing at her feet. "This guy, well, a customer called me two days ago." she shifted nervously. "He asked me to do something for him. Which I had done without knowing what it was he wanted." She glanced at the door and breathed in deeply.

"He is trying to blame me for everything. I only did what he asked, though."

As she spoke, I noticed her demeanor changing. Her shoulders sagged, and she hung her head against her chest. Jamie sat with her hands folded in her lap. She looked defeated, and I felt sorry for her. However, if she had what I thought, she could be a benefit. That information would be like holding precious gems. Keeping her safe would be easy.

"Tell me about you, you from around here?" I inquired watching her every move.

Jamie blinked and turned her head to the side as she responded. "Kind of. I have lived in Miami most of my life but not in this territory in another part on the other side."

"And you came all this way on your own for protection you say?" I wondered how far she had actually come. Judging by her appearance she had surely spent a day or two on the run.

"I was heading," she rubbed her cheek as if in thought formulating her answer. "Heading to another place but couldn't stay there."

"So, the danger you are in can come looking for you here then?" I inquired, wondering how many groups were after her.

"I--I don't know," she said softly.

"Give me a second to consider what you are asking," I said as I stood and walked to the door. Opening the door, I waved the guard closer. "Please take her to the back dressing room," I told him as he approached me.

"Jamie," I stated, looking at her. She rose and turned to me. "He will show you to the back, get cleaned, and see if any clothing hanging there fits you. You can't go around looking like that. Put on some other clothes. I'll be back shortly."

She nodded and left with him. I headed upstairs to my office. I called Leo and informed him that I may have a lead on the hacker, but I would let him know if the information panned out. Sitting back in my chair, I consider my options. I liked her spunk and fighting attitude.

Maybe I could turn this into a win-win situation, but I had to be sure. She needed to be protected, and what she could do if she was the hacker, would be useful. How would I make it work though? And then it struck me, the perfect solution. This would get the family off my back, sort out Ana and give me a solid hold on her.

I called down and ordered some food and more coffee. I told the guard to bring her up once she was done. We could continue our chat in my office now. Comfortable enough with my decision, I waited.

The food came shortly before Jamie did. As she entered, I felt my chest tightening. Dressed in a tight-fitting pair of blue jeans, the neon light from the signs streaming in through the window cast a fantastic glow upon her.

Her silky-smooth skin, now clearly visible, highlighted her sparkling blue eyes. She was a vision to behold. The white lacey top she wore surely made her breasts more noticeable as well. Jamie looked nothing like the woman who had entered here a couple of hours ago.

I was frozen in time for a moment, speechless, as I struggled to regain my senses. I cleared my throat before speaking. "Well, you clean up nicely," I said, waving my hand and pointing to the chair. "Sit, I ordered some food as I am sure you must be hungry."

Jamie faintly smiled and sat down. I couldn't take my eyes off her. "I think we can make some kind of arrangement," I said, sipping some coffee.

"Thank you," she blurted out. Grinning as she took one of the pizza rounds and started eating.

I watched her finish it before continuing. "Right, so, to keep you safe, we would have to do it a bit differently than usual, but I feel confident we can assist each other." I started as I took a slice from the plate.

Jamie wiped her mouth and raised her eyebrows at me. After drinking some coffee, she spoke. "So, tell me how you can keep me safe and what I have to do in return?"

"You have to look at it from our point of view," I said, once I swallowed the bite I took. I studied her reaction as I spoke. She shifted slightly on the chair and placed the cup down.

"Your point of view," Jamie stated. "And what is that?"

I could see she was suddenly uncomfortable. But I rather enjoyed seeing her squirm. "My proposition may sound a bit far-fetched. But I assure you it is the only way." I spoke deliberately, slowly, hoping she would accept what I was about to say. I was still processing my idea but knew it would be the best option.

Jamie stared at me blankly. Folding my hands, I placed them on my table and leaned forward. "I can offer you full protection, but you will have to marry me." Before I could continue, Jamie rose to her feet.

She gasped loudly. "You are unbelievable." She spat at me. "Who do you think I am?"

"Please sit down, I'm not done," I responded calmly. She was fiery as she flopped back onto the chair. She mumbled to herself, looking at the wall.

If she was who I thought, she would have no other options. She was stunning, intelligent and wild. I was sure she would be a preferred choice where the family was concerned in comparison to Ana.

"Jamie," I said, waiting for her to look at me. "If you want our protection, this is what is needed. But," I added, taking a deep breath. "You will also bear me a child in exchange for protection. Being married to me gives you all the protection you will need and for some form of freedom, you will bear me a child."

Jamie's mouth fell open, and her eyes widened. I sat back, allowing it all to sink in. Feeling proud of myself. I was killing two birds with one stone. I would give the family valuable information. Luder and Leo can stop complaining about my escapades. Plus, I could get Ana off my back without banishing her from the organization.

I had asked Ana to marry me two years back but the family made it clear that she would not be accepted. Ever since my brother fell in love with his better half, he started embracing this idea of *the one*. Like I cared finding the one. My arrangement with Ana worked well—she worked for us, we fucked and then we went separate ways. Hence, I had struggled somewhat with their ultimatum but eventually accepted it, because, after all, I didn't really care all that much.

However, this woman before me was more in line with what they expected. There's also something about her I couldn't really name. Most of all though, I was thinking logically about it and not falling head over heels like my brother. This was a solid business transaction with some benefits.

"Look, you need to decide now. It's not that I want to pressure you. But my offer is only available for now. Once we leave here, it expires."

Grinning, I rose and headed for the door. "You have until I return," I stated, leaving quickly to check in with the guards. She had a lot to think of and I was sure she could do with some time to consider her options.

Ana's pride might be hurt at first, but she was strong and would bounce back as always. After all, it wasn't like I was throwing her to the curb, she could stay in her position. I was simply making a strategical move that would benefit the family.

Heading back downstairs I grinned widely as I felt like a cheshire cat who had just received a bowl of cream for being a good boy. I needed to let the guards know that she wasn't to leave the premises under any circumstances. If she decided not to take my offer, I would escort her out myself.

Chapter 5 - Jamie

Shocked to the core, I watched him leave the room. He must be insane if he thought I would accept such an offer. Standing, I walked to the large window. Looking out over the city, I breathed out loudly.

"Marriage?" I uttered. "What is this guy thinking?" Placing my hands on the window frame, I leaned forward. My mind was whirling. Even considering this was preposterous. I closed my eyes and felt the warm breeze cool the sweat on my forehead. How dare he, I thought, feeling my anger rising. Just then my phone vibrated in my pocket before I could formulate any reasoning.

As I pulled it from my pocket, I turned and leaned against the windowsill. There was a new message. Opening it, I saw it was Pedro.

There was an address, and the message read: *Meet me here in an hour. You must keep your promise. The enemies are searching and closing in. I know where you are. I will keep you safe but don't disappoint me, sugar.*

Keep me safe, I thought. Look what you have brought me, my life, for safety. What kind of safety is this? Then I shivered, thinking about Pedro's hands all over me. I didn't want this, and I didn't want to sleep with him. Sliding down the wall, I felt my heart beating faster. A lump formed in my throat. I didn't want to die either.

As I sat there, I felt the first tear slip from my eye. It rolled down my cheek slowly as my heart sank to my feet. I lowered my head between my knees. I had no choice. I would have to marry this man. If I didn't, he would surely throw me out and where would I go then?

This thought brought an image of me and Pedro hiding out. I suddenly felt sick, he was a truly ugly man with broken teeth and rotting breath. If I wasn't so drunk the first time, it would never have happened.

Under any other circumstances, I wouldn't even consider this an option. In fact, I would have laughed this Ashan guy off. He wasn't the kind of man I would be seen with not that I was sure what kind of man I wanted. At this stage of my life, I was focusing on me and getting my life together.

"You did a swell job of that, Jamie," I said out loud as pain streamed up my tight shoulders into my neck. My head felt like it was swelling as tears burned my eyes.

But being honest with myself, except for the obvious reasons. There was something about him, though. When he entered the room, I felt a strange pull. There was a pounding at the walls I had built, weakening them. His aura attracted me, and I wanted to know more about him, but I wasn't sure this was the way.

Taking a deep breath and wiping my eyes, I thought about my options. There were three options. Leave and take my chances alone out there, go to Pedro or marry Ashan.

I glanced up as the door opened. Ashan strolled in and stood next to the table, looking down at me. "Have you come to a conclusion?" he asked.

Pushing up against the wall, I rose to my feet. Meeting his eyes, I slowly nodded as I answered. "Yes, my answer is y--yes." My whole being screamed as I spoke, but I knew this might be my only safe option. I didn't dare go out there alone and Pedro wasn't even on the cards.

Ashan's grin lit up his entire face as he replied. "Good choice. Right, we will be married right away then. But first, you should shower and clean properly."

Shocked at the urgency he showed but also relieved in a way, I simply nodded. No words could ever portray what I felt inside. This would be a temporary thing, I thought, I would get myself out of this somehow.

"Come, come," Ashan continued as he walked back to the door. Holding it open, he waved for me to exit the office with him. "I'll take you up to my suite, where you can have a shower. While you do that, I'll get everything ready." He suddenly sounded light. If he had smiled, I would have known he was happy, but his face remained straight.

I followed quietly as he led me down a passage to a reasonably large room. It was pretty bare except for two luxurious couches. In one corner stood an old oak desk with a computer on it, and in another corner was what appeared to be a small serving station. It had a couple of cups, a kettle, and tins which I presumed held coffee, tea, and sugar.

There were no decorations and the room felt cold. Almost void of life. How could anyone live like this? I felt a sliver of fear run down my spine as he ushered me through a door to the left of the empty room. There were no cupboards or shelves in this empty room. No portraits, photos, or even books.

The brown walls and red carpet filled the room with a strange darkness. Ashan opened the door before me to the left and pushed me inside. I felt my anger wanting to surface as I was being led and pushed around like an animal heading for slaughter.

Turning to face him, I wanted to protest. Yet, his green eyes appeared to have a spark in them, turning his hard look soft. As he spoke, I could hear a tenderness in his voice. "Right, you have a shower while I get things set up."

Still tired and sore, I asked pleadingly, "Could I get some sleep in first?"

"Once it's over you can get some," he calmly replied. "I promise to make it quick and painless."

Knowing I had no choice, I nodded and waited for him to close the bathroom door. As the door closed, I turned to study the bathroom. It was astonishing, a total contrast to the other room. The bathroom looked like something you would see in a high-end fashion magazine. I felt my breath catch as I studied it.

The biggest tub I'd ever seen sat to my left, and next to it was the shower. These two were huge and took up half the space. The shower had double glass doors. On the hooks next to the doors hung thick and fluffy robes. Stepping closer, I felt the material. It was so soft I couldn't wait to wrap it around me. I had never felt something quite so luxurious. I quickly undressed and stepped into the shower. It was like walking into a fairytale.

The walls, floor, and ceiling were covered in images of a forest. Before me, the wall displayed a realistic waterfall. To the sides were lush green forests. It was breathtaking. Opening the mixer tap, nozzles sprayed water from all sides. I couldn't help but giggle as the lukewarm water greeted my skin. Turning in circles filled with excitement, I forgot all my problems for a moment.

I was enthralled by the staggering charm of the shower, feeling like a princess out in the wilderness. Who was this man, I wondered as I took a sponge from the shelve. There was an array of sponges and soaps to pick and choose from. After smelling all the soaps, I selected one that complimented the forest theme. It had an herbal earthy aroma with a hint of wildflowers.

Closing my eyes as I covered my skin in silky smooth bubbles, I breathed in deeply. My mind traveled far away from all the troubles on the other side of the door. Feeling the strain leaving my body, I wished I could stay in the shower forever. Any one that shared the kind of live I had lived would surely have grabbed such an invitation with open arms.

Yet, I have seen people like these, read many more articles online and knew the lives of the rich wasn't as cosher as they made it sound. Especially when it came to Bratva. These people would kill you for looking at them funny.

Grinning at myself, I wondered if that was true and how they took rejection. Turning in slow circles I thought back at all the oldies I have watched with mafia in. It all seemed surreal until you stepped into one. I felt like I was watching a movie of myself.

But reality snuck back in as I heard a commotion in the other room. There were a couple of voices, but I couldn't make out what they were saying. After quickly washing my hair and rinsing, I stepped out.

Wrapping the fluffy robe around me, I walked to the door. Placing my ear up against it, I listened. All was suddenly quiet on the other side. Opening the door slowly, I peek into the room. It was empty; there was no one there. I wondered if I was hearing voices in my head from all the stress of the last couple of days.

Grinning to myself, I stepped into the room. My eyes fell on the computer just sitting on the bare table. The screen was giving off a bright light. It was off earlier but now it was on. Someone had been in here while I was showering. Carefully, I walked towards it. I listened for any sound outside, but everything was quiet.

Sitting down at the desk, I felt my heart rate quicken. Shaking my hands out and twisting my head left and right, I prepared to deep dive into his files. I had to know who he was. Seeing that there were no photos or other clues anywhere, I would do it with a quick search. Placing my fingers on the keyboard, I filled with excitement. "What will I find?" I whispered as I started my search.

As I opened one file after another, I smiled, feeling alive. The system lacked security, and I breezed through it without hassle. This was my passion, but my smile faded rapidly as I opened a 'Family' file. Rising swiftly, I felt the chair pushing back a bit too quickly; it toppled over, landing with a loud banging sound.

"No, no, no," I exhaled deeply, glancing around the room and at the chair. He wasn't just a manager, as I had thought. Staring at the screen wide-eyed, I pushed my hands through my hair. He was one of the Morozov family.

I thought he only worked here, running the business for them. I had no idea that he was a Morozov. This changed everything. I couldn't stay. Stepping back, I picked up the chair and pushed it back to the table. I had to get out; marrying him was no longer an option. With him knowing what I had done, there was only one reason why he would want to marry me.

My mind raced a hundred miles an hour. Sprinting back to the bathroom, I dressed hastily as I needed to get out before he returned. Exiting the bathroom, I headed for the door. I would sneak out and run, I thought.

Yet, as I touched the handle, the wall parted next to the door, opening into a secret room. Ashan stepped out, grabbed my hands, and swung me around. He moved in and pinned me to the door, pushing my hands up above my head.

He was a tall muscular man and I felt tiny against him. Looking up at him, he was grinning. His eyes reflected his strength and dedication. My stomach turned as his expression changed. I didn't know what he was thinking, but I had an intense need to try to rectify the situation. I didn't know I was being watched.

"And now the sudden rush?" Ashan asked. His voice sounded calm but had a tinge of sarcasm or anger, I couldn't be sure.

My nerves tingled, and so did my skin, where he held me. I was sure it wasn't only from how he looked at me. But being up close, feeling his hands on me, absorbing his strong aroma was indeed messing with my mind. His grasp was like that of an old friend and made me uneasy.

"I was going to look for you," I uttered, trying to pull my eyes from his. I felt trapped, yet I couldn't look away. He smelled of peppermint and honey. His touch was gentle but firm. My eyes toured down his strong cheekbones to his slightly parted lips. They appeared soft and supple, inviting.

Suddenly, I had to fight the urge to kiss him. My body was reacting to the chemistry developing between us. We were planets from different dimensions on a collision course. Leaning my head back against the door, I closed my eyes for a second.

I had to get a grip on the emotions surging through my body. What was happening? This man was powerful, handsome, and so wrong for me. I didn't fit into this world, I couldn't be a showpiece, I was from another class.

It could never work, I assured myself, opening my eyes again. His stare made me uncomfortable, but his silence was worse. I wondered what he was thinking and felt fear creeping in. What was he going to do?

"You found what you were looking for?" he asked, leaning in. His voice was low and sounded deeper than before. His hot breath softly touching my cheek caused a tumbling in my stomach. I had to get a grip on my emotions, but I had nowhere to go. I struggled a bit but stopped as the movement only caused my senses to absorb more of him.

My body jolted as feelings of excitement and danger crawled up my back. I was suddenly hot as adrenaline ran rampage through my senses.

"Well," I started saying. Pulling my eyes away and staring over his shoulder, I swallowed hard. "It wasn't like you gave me another option. You didn't tell me you are part of the Morozov family."

Regaining some of my composure, I glanced back at him. I could only hope that my look was filled with resolve and didn't show the sudden onset of lust I felt surging through me. "I have a right to know who I am marrying, don't I?"

He didn't say a word. He smiled and nodded. I had to get a hold on myself. He was so wrong for me and these feelings although new, weren't what I expected. I didn't know if it was due to the danger he portrayed or the need for a man but I couldn't trust my body or mind at the moment.

CHAPTER 6 - ASHAN

Pressed up against her, I felt a surge of power run through me. I had never met anyone who made me think about certain things in life, and I didn't know why she did, but she did. Her presence filled me with a drive I had not felt in years. My mind kept telling me to slow down but my body wanted her more than the air I breathed.

Watching her work with so much restless sort of energy only made me want to learn more about her. I needed to keep her close; I had to protect her and what she had. Not only the information I was sure the family would want, but also her talent, drive, and energy.

Jamie was competent and resourceful. Noting her strong will, my mind ran in a different direction. I wonder if she did everything in life with the same kind of energy. If so, I imagined sex with her would be phenomenal. This thought invaded my mind like an unexpected rocket.

Leaning closer, I lowered my tone as I spoke. "You are something else."

If I seduced her, I was sure to unlock the tigress she held inside. Judging from the clothing she came in with, I felt sure she did not have many suitors. I could teach her so much in life and in bed, of this, I was sure.

Feeling certain of myself, I studied her face as she battled to look away over my shoulder before replying. Her skin felt like velvet where I held her. She smelled of wildflowers and oak, prickling my senses.

"I don't see what difference my last name makes," I whispered as I pressed harder against her. This allowed my one hand freedom from holding her pinned. With my free hand, I made soft lines down her arm with my fingertip.

She breathed in sharply as I placed a tender kiss on her neck. Holding her wrists, I pulled her arms further up over her head and pinned them solidly to the door. Jamie shivered against me. I gently pushed my foot between her legs. As I moved my knee left and right, opening her legs, her breathing became uneven.

She tensed as I pressed harder up against her. Moving my hand from her shoulder down, my fingers filled with heat as I moved in between and then over her firm breast. An intense desire started pushing up in me, but I have always had exceptional control and wasn't worried.

Moving further down, I grabbed her butt with force. Jamie trembled slightly. Her breathing turned quick and hot. I fully intended to seduce her, but I felt my control slivering away as she filled my ear with soft breaths. Taking back control, I had to step away.

I walked over to the desk and shook off the bubbling emotions that were making their way up. Turning off the computer, I glanced at her as I spoke. "At least put on the dress I hung in the bathroom for you, if you don't mind."

Jamie quietly retired to the bathroom and closed the door. Straightening, I shook out my arms. Closing my eyes, I tried to clear my mind. The goal was to seduce her, not the other way around. I had to get a grip on my emotions, or my plans with her might fail like my deal did. Thinking about the deal was all I needed to clear the cobwebs forming in my mind.

A knock at the door brought me from my thoughts. Opening it, I invited the officiator in. "Welcome, and thanks for coming so quickly," I said, walking to the bathroom door. I knocked and called out to her. "Jamie, it's time."

"Coming," she replied through the closed door.

I hoped that the dress I had brought up would fit her. On such short notice, it was the only thing I could find in the dancer's fitting room that seemed appropriate. It wasn't a wedding gown, but it was as close as I could get, and I hoped she liked it.

Walking back to the officiate, I heard the door opening behind me. Standing in front of him, I turned and looked back at her.

Jamie came out of the bathroom wearing the pearl evening gown. She lit up the room as she moved. The dress was a perfect fit, better than perfect. Her perky breasts were pushed up in the tight V running down between them, covered in lace. The skirt hugged her curves just enough, making them clearly visible. She was slim but curvy in all the right places.

I swallowed hard as she looked like she was gliding towards us. Sweat broke out on the back of my neck, and it felt as if my tie was trying to strangle me. She was a vision to behold. I was wrong earlier when I thought she looked perfect in the jeans and white top. This dress made her look like an exquisite gem. I couldn't help but notice the grin forming as she came to stand beside me.

My hands were sweaty, and my mouth kept filling with spit as I admired her. I didn't know that any woman could be so desirable. I have never encountered one that made all my senses light up, and she did. It was new to me, and I tried to not show the impact she had on me. Clearing my throat, I nodded to the officiate to proceed. I dared not speak as I was sure my voice would betray me.

The ceremony went quickly, as I had arranged beforehand. We only needed the most important aspects covered. After the final 'I do's,' we exchanged plain wedding bands, which I had one of the guards get for me.

I leaned in for a quick kiss. Jamie's lips were soft and warm, sending fire through my senses. Pulling back, I noticed a shine in her eyes as she lowered her head quickly, but not quickly enough.

She was either excited and glowing or she felt broken and was about to cry. I needed to find out. Walking to the door with the officiate, I glanced back. Jamie just stood there, not moving.

As the officiate left, one of my guards entered. He quietly informed me of a development that had to be dealt with. Frustrated at the disruption, I walked over to Jamie. Taking her by the shoulders, I ushered her to the suite through the door at the back next to the bathroom. Entering the suite, I close the door behind us.

My body was screaming for her touch, I breathed in deeply, needing to calm myself. I spoke to her as she surveyed the lavish suite. "Jamie, this is my home and now yours as well." I started. "To the back on the right is the kitchen. The furthest door here on the left leads to the bathroom."

Taking her hand, I turned her to face me. "Jamie, do you understand?" I asked. She appeared to be in a daze, and I was sure everything was a bit overwhelming.

"I have to leave now as something has come up that needs my attention," I added. "You can have that sleep now and I'll be back as soon as possible."

Jamie nodded slowly. I felt a bit uneasy as she showed no apparent reaction. I had no idea what she was thinking or feeling, but I couldn't stay.

Walking to the door, I glanced back as I spoke again. "Jamie, I am locking the door for your own safety. I promise I will be back shortly, get comfortable, hun, okay."

She just stood there looking around. Leaving the suite, I locked the door and locked the bathroom door on this side as well. Once I felt sure she couldn't get out and no one could get in, I headed down to see what was going on.

As I went down, I convinced myself I was doing all I could to protect her. At some point, I would have to inform the family as well. But for now, it would be better if no one knew. This way, she wasn't in any danger. Not that the family would place her in danger, but the less people knew about her whereabouts, the better.

Leo knew I suspected that the hacker had come here for protection. But marrying her, I wasn't even sure I knew what I was doing. They would call me crazy, but I did what I thought to be right in the moment.

In time, I would explain my actions to them and to her. Maybe I just wanted someone as well, as Leo and Luder kept reminding me; I wasn't sure what had made me decide to marry her and demand a child. But what was done was done.

Chapter 7 - Jamie

Hearing the key turning in the door pulled me from the sudden daze and frozenness. It all happened so quickly, I was still trying to make sense of it as he left and locked the door. I went from dressing in this gown to married, and now being locked up all in a question of minutes.

"He locked the door," I breathed out, realizing what had just happened. How dare he lock me in? What or who did he think I was? How was he to decide what was needed, I married him as he asked; locking me in wasn't part of the deal. Feeling my blood boil as my anger rose, I stepped to the door and tried the handle.

I was astounded to find it was indeed locked. I banged on the door for a bit, but no one came. Turning back, I stood against it as I studied the suite again. It was lavish and quite large, like the bathroom. But I was trapped like an animal. My fingernails dug into my palms from the tightness of my fists as I tried to control my anger.

The veins in my neck pumped, and my head felt like it was about to explode. Controlling my rage has never been one of my strong points. I was furious at him for locking me in but also at myself. It wasn't my fault that I was in this situation, though. Why did I have to pay for doing what was asked of me?

"I will get you, Ben, and clear my name," I screamed at the room. Taking a couple of deep breaths, I vowed to get him and get out of this stupid marriage as soon as possible. But first things first. Feeling a bit calmer, I decided to see what the suite held and what was at my disposal. Even though I was still tired and sore, I focused on what was before me.

The room seemed to have more than the two doors Ashan mentioned. The current room I found myself in appeared to be a bedroom/living room. Against the back was a king-size bed, and two double chaise chairs and a large TV were before them.

I noticed no windows in the room, so it had to be a center room, and the others may have windows. The decor was a deep red and black. If not for all the lights, I imagined it could get pretty dark in here. Next to the bed in the right-hand corner against the back wall was a closed door, which he hadn't mentioned.

On my right was one open door, which I assumed was the kitchen, and another closed door. To the left were two closed doors, one of which had to be the bathroom.

Walking to the left, I felt the first door. It opened into the bathroom as expected. The other door next to it, however, was locked. Moving across the room, I felt the other two closed doors. No surprise there; both were locked as well. Both the bathroom and kitchen didn't have any windows either. I was locked in, but Ashan didn't know me that well.

Moving into the small sparking kitchen, I wondered if he even cooked. It was fitted with all the amenities one could need. Yet, the fridge, dishwasher, microwave, oven, toaster, kettle, and other equipment were all silver and appeared brand new. I supposed with a restaurant and kitchen at your disposal, no one ever needed to cook.

The walls and cupboards had a marble look, and even the cutlery and dinnerware appeared brand new. It all looked untouched as if no one had ever lived here.

As I went through the last cupboard, there was a knock at the door. I peeked around the kitchen doorway as the suite door opened. A couple of women entered; some pushed trolleys with food, and others carried in boxes.

Stepping into the room, the women all looked at me. Most nodded, smiled, placed down what they had, and left. One woman remained as the others left, and I walked over to see what they had brought.

"Hi, I'm Ana," the curious woman beside me said. Her red locks fell softly down her back and over her shoulders. Yet, there was something in her pasted-on smile I couldn't quite place.

"Hi, Jamie," I replied, holding out my hand. Ana looked at it as if I had some kind of virus. Stepping back, she turned and pointed at the boxes and trolleys instead as she spoke. "There are about ten meals for you to choose from. You can also save some if you want in the fridge. Just send back what you don't want."

Caught a bit off guard, I didn't respond. This didn't seem to faze Ana in any way as she strolled to the bathroom door. Stopping in the doorway, she looked back at me before speaking. "In the bathroom are closets. The boxes contain clothing. If they don't fit or you don't want them, send them back. The ones you decide to keep..." She trailed off as she pointed to the bathroom.

Grinning, Ana spoke in a slightly pitched voice as she came back towards me. "A new sparkling toy is all you are to him, you know." She flopped herself down on the chaise, comfortable as can be, before continuing. "He's a beast in bed," she added, tapping her nails on the side of the chaise." He's going to enjoy breaking you in but will return to me."

My anger ignited again as she spoke. Who did she think she was making such snide comments and taunting me? I felt sure if he wanted her, he would have married her. Ana rose and glided past me to the door.

Before leaving, she spoke out again. "He can fulfill your wildest fantasies if you let him. Enjoy it while you can." She closed the door and locked it. Out of anger at her, I threw one of the boxes at the door. Clothing spilled from it to the floor.

It was sweet that he delivered all these things: food, clothing, and everything I needed. Yet, there was no phone or laptop anywhere.

As I collected the clothing and placed it back in the box, I found my mind traveling to his hold and hot lips. Annoyed at myself for allowing my mind to go there, I placed the box back with the others. I felt sure that night had now turned into day, or maybe all the activities and dark room had me confused. Feeling my body weakened and overcome with fatigue, I knew I needed to sleep. Placing the food in the fridge, I lay down on the bed.

Waking sometime later, I was still alone. I didn't know if it was still night or the next day. Being in the darkness without windows was messing with my internal clock. After making some coffee in his new kitchen, I started going through the boxes of clothing as I ate some of the cold food.

I searched through the clothing, dressed in something more comfortable, and also found something I wasn't looking for. Sitting back with the hairpins in hand, I glanced at the locked doors.

Unlocking all the other doors, I could go anywhere, I thought. Glancing into each room, I decided to explore the biggest one first. As far as I could see, all the rooms were neat and organized. They also held multiple other doors, which I would get to in time.

Most, like the one we came in through, had minimal decor. Some tables and chairs, another held a wall-to-wall monitor or TV, and the biggest one had only a couple of chairs with what looked like a massage bed. He sure had a strange nature I thought.

Unlocking the doors that led out of this room brought with them some secrets. There was a small dark room with only a single chair and what looked like an old radio. Sitting down, I stared at the device on the small round table.

Reaching out, I jumped in the chair, letting out a tiny scream as voices filled the room. It sounded like some of the staff, but I couldn't be sure. It sounded like Ana barking orders. Turning the dial more, I found silence, then what sounded like fans blowing and some voices again. The voices in this setting were all new to me.

It could be the guards, I thought as I listened. Suddenly, I heard Ashan's voice. I was frightened but listened for a bit before turning off the device and leaving the room. If he caught me snooping, he might get angry, and even though I didn't know what he would do, being locked up was bad enough for me.

The next room I opened looked like a big entertainment area. In the middle stood a large round wooden table; counting the chairs, there was seating for twelve. One wall was lined with shelves and cupboards. On the other side stood an old protector.

I felt sure it was most likely for family meetings and not entertainment. Baking out of the room, I closed the door and made sure it was locked. I was convinced Ashan wouldn't appreciate me sneaking around there.

Moving to the last door, I glanced around nervously. I couldn't be sure when he would be back, but I didn't want him finding me all over his place. I hadn't found windows in any of these rooms or phones, and it was puzzling. Unlocking the last door, I opened it quickly and stepped into the room, needing to see what was in it before heading back to the main suite.

Doing so, I crashed into what felt like a hard wall. Yet, it wasn't a wall at all. Raising my hands to his chest, I pushed myself back from the brick of a man before me. At first, I thought it was one of the guards. Looking up as I walked backward, I met Ashan's gaze.

I had entered his office unknowingly through a side door. This room had the windows, a phone, and a computer I was seeking. But it also had Ashan. The look on this face was positively murderous.

Not knowing anything about him, I gasped as fear stepped in.

"I was on my way back," he spat at me. "What in heaven's name are you doing here? How did you even get here?" He continued as he stepped towards me while I walked backward. I could hear the anger in his voice and tried retreating quicker. But he was on me like lightning.

Grabbing me by the arm, he stepped forward and slammed the door behind him. He shoved it so hard that I swore it vibrated the entire wall.

CHAPTER 8 - ASHAN

I knew the door to my right came down from the suite, and no one had access. It was locked from the inside, and I had the only key from this side. Hearing the door unlocking pulled me out from behind my table. Walking around to the door, I picked up the bat Luder had given me a couple of years back.

He had it signed for me by the entire Marlin's team. It was the only thing that could be used as a weapon, as my guns were locked in the safe. There was no time to get them out before that door would open. Glancing at the bat, I hoped I wouldn't need to use it.

I stood before the door, waiting for whoever was on the other side to enter. There had been some break-ins a while back. So, I had installed extra rooms and protocols to try and figure out who or what was going on. I had to see if the break-ins were inside jobs or outsiders.

This door led to more than just my suite. None of my staff knew about it as far as I was concerned. Hearing the lock turning placed me on edge, but I was ready for whoever was snooping around my den.

Jamie was the last person I expected to come through the door and into my office. I locked her in my suite the previous night and would have been up sooner, but I had some drunks making a scene to handle. Then, some of the machines broke down, and the night just kept giving.

It was a long night, and I was tired, but we had only now gotten all the situations under control, and everything was running again. I felt relief and anger passing through me as she opened the door and walked through it.

"Are you trying to escape?" I breathed out as Jamie emerged from the door slamming into me. She tried retreating, but I was on her quickly. Grabbing her arm, I pulled her around and pushed her into the chair. Locking the door, I felt my anger rising.

"What in heaven's name," I shouted as I turned to her.

Grabbing her by the arm, and pulling her up out of the chair, I stormed out of my office. I pulled her back to the suite with me. "I would have been up in a bit. I was just handling some issues. Why weren't you sleeping instead of snooping?" I shouted as we moved. I was filled with rage. How dare she try escaping with all I was doing for her?

Entering the suite, I pushed her to the bed in anger and disappointment. I opened the fridge and noticed most of the food hadn't been touched. The boxes of clothing were still in the middle of the floor as well. "What more do you want from me?" I hollered at her as I locked the door she tried to escape through.

"I sent up food and clothing, and you weren't even interested?" I queried, waving at the boxes and pointing at the fridge. "I married you for your safety and offered you a part of my life, and this is the thanks I get? Are you running off?"

She just sat there staring at me, her face blank of any emotion. Yet, that spark I saw the previous day flickered in her eyes. As I walked to her, she started moving back on the bed. "Speak to me, tell me what you were doing?" I blared at her.

Jamie cleared her throat, glanced at the fridge and boxes, and then looked me in the eyes as she spoke. "I wasn't trying to escape; I was exploring." She stated calmly but firmly. There was something in her tone I couldn't quite place, though. Anger, disappointment, I couldn't pin it. So, I waited for her to finish.

"I hate, no, I don't like being locked up. I need space and fresh air." She waved her hand through the air as she continued. "There's no windows in this place. If you deny me space and air," she stopped, got up, and stepped closer.

"If you do that," she continued, tapping me on the chest. "You're a bigger jerk than I imagined." She turned and folded her arms across her chest. She was so perfectly formed. Staring at her tiny middle, big hips, and ass, my mouth filled with spit as I felt heat rising inside.

Her confidence drove my senses wild. My body lit up like a firecracker as I watched her. I felt my heart pounding in my chest as heat surged through me. This fiery side of her was a big turn-on for me. Plus, she's one of a handful of people to ever stand up against me.

I vowed silently that I had to have her, had to make her mine. Stepping closer, I turned her around to face me. She placed both her hands on my chest as I moved in. "Jamie," I whispered, feeling my anger being replaced by a strong yearning for her.

Her touch, feeling her hands on my chest, stocked the fire even more. Shimmering just below the surface was a hunger I never knew I possessed.

My dick had awakened and was throbbing as I reached out to pull her in. As my fingers touched her hips, Jamie pushed me away. "No," she spat at me, turning and walking to the other side of the room.

Watching her walk away only increased my desire. As I followed her, she turned and stretched out her hands before her. "No," she repeated sharply. "I refuse to be with you as long as you are actively still fucking other women."

Astounded by her accusation, I stopped and studied her wondering where she got that idea from. Everything about her, her stance, words, and look, screamed at me. I knew the fight had turned her on as well. Her blue eyes were dark as the ocean on a stormy night and her voice betrayed her as it dripped with sweet lust. I just needed to find a way in.

"I'm not having sex with anyone at the moment," I breathed out as I stepped in closer, allowing her hands to heat my chest again. "Jamie, I don't know what you heard, but there is no one in my life at this time," I whispered, taking hold of her hands.

Pulling her hands up to my mouth, I gently kissed her fingers and felt the stiffness dissipate from her arms. "But that woman," she started saying as I leaned in. Her eyes were fiery, and her breath hot. As our lips were about to meet, there was a knock at the door.

I wanted to scream and beat whoever was on the other side to a pulp. But I knew that would drive a wedge here and I wanted her to want me. Breathing loudly, I let her hands go as I turned and walked briskly to the door. I stood for a second, breathing sharply to calm my hormones before opening the door.

Opening it, I found my head bodyguard on the other side. "Yes," I breathed out loudly, glancing back at Jamie. She was still standing where I left her, and I wanted to get back there as quickly as possible. My mind filled with visions of her naked on the bed, ready for the taking.

"Sorry to disturb boss," he replied calmly. "I came to let you know that the client has arrived early. We have set them up in the booth as instructed."

I nodded as he spoke, knowing that this with Jamie would have to wait again. Closing my eyes, I breathed in deeply again. I didn't want to leave her. I wanted to stay and fuck her brains out. But this meeting was vital. I couldn't let the clients wait. "Okay, thanks, I'll be down shortly," I replied before closing the door. I softly slammed my fist up against it before turning to face Jamie.

"Is this client, the one where the sale is still hinging on the dead guy?" she asked as I walked closer.

"The what?" I questioned, astounded by her remark.

"Yeah," she replied, grinning. "As I was exploring, I heard some chatter about a sale that didn't go through. It had something to do with a dead guy everyone was looking for."

Jamie sat back down on the side of the bed, seemingly calmer. She was more intelligent than I thought. I didn't dare let her out of sight yet. Keeping her close could prove beneficial. She had more skills than I knew about.

"Jamie," I said, holding out my hand. "How about you join me tonight? I am sure you can assist me. Plus, it would give you an opportunity to get out of the room."

Jamie beamed as she rose sharply and took my hand. "Yes, please, anything but this suite. What would you like me to do?" Her touch was soft and for a moment, I considered letting the client wait. Shaking the cobwebs loose, I focused on what had to be done.

"Right, find something dazzling to wear in the boxes I sent up. Glam yourself up and then come down to find me. You could listen to our conversation and maybe pick up something about the client. And then you can let me know what you think."

"I can do that, yes," she replied eagerly.

Walking to the door as she started opening boxes I wondered if this was a good idea. But, I had to find out how much worth she held and this would be a good time to test my theory.

"Don't take too long, please," I added as I left her rummaging through the clothes. Closing the door but leaving it unlocked, I headed down to meet the client. Jamie might be able to offer me more than I originally thought. Keeping her with me would be better for us both, and there would be no need for her snooping.

She wasn't only beautiful but had a lot more to offer than I could ever have imagined. I just knew the family would love her. Swiping all these thoughts from my mind, I entered the booth to sit with the client, hoping she would be down soon.

CHAPTER 9 - JAMIE

Rummaging through the boxes in search of something I would look good in but also be comfortable wearing was a task. My nerves lumped in my shoulders, but my stomach turned excitedly. I felt like a spy in a movie and would play my part with grace. Ashan drove me wild simply by the way he looked at me. There was a hunger in his eyes and his sudden mood changes were something I wasn't used to.

As I went, I threw clothes left and right. Opening the fourth box, I froze. Lifting the skimpy, glittering black number up, I gasped. This was it, I thought as I held it up against me. It was just long enough to hide what needed to remain unseen but short enough to entice the audience.

Confident that I could make this look work, I dressed quickly. In another box, I found makeup and hair accessories. I pinned some of my hair up and allowed some to frame my face. After applying a light coating of makeup, I admired my new look in the life-size mirror. I had never worn make-up but felt sure the bit of blush, mascara and lipstick I added was sufficient.

Pushing out my lips, I kissed the mirror. "Perfect," I whispered to my reflection. The dress revealed the right amount of cleavage if you asked me. It sat halfway up above my knee and the high heels popped out my calves.

Even though I preferred to stay hidden and cover up everything, I was thrilled to see the reaction of the men downstairs. Thinking back to Ashan's reaction of me in the evening dress, I was sure he would appreciate it. Plus, I had never worn anything like this before, but I had seen movies where women wore these kinds of dresses.

Turning as I moved to the door, I could see the headlines. I would have been a perfect spy in another life. After my earlier tricks, I knew that most places couldn't keep me contained and people generally underestimated me.

After a couple of steps left and right in the room, I found my footing and felt comfortable in the heels. Pleased with myself, I headed downstairs. Blending in as one of the club workers, I searched for Ashan and the client. As I neared the furthest side of the bar, I saw them in the last private booth.

Ashan seemed to have a glow about him. He was explaining something to the client. His smile spread across his face like I have not yet seen.

Grabbing a tray with drinks from the bar counter, I headed over. I slowly entered, holding out the tray of drinks while listening to their conversation. I was hoping to gather information that may come in handy later. Ashan had said I should listen, and I was doing so. I wanted to prove my worth to him and maybe I could get out of this marriage sooner.

The client was an elderly man. I suspected he was in his late forties or early fifties. His companion was a stocky man about half his age. Leaning forward, I held the drinks tray out to them first. They each took a glass and thanked me. The client also winked at me with a grin that made me shiver slightly.

His shining black suit looked a size too small if you asked me. His slicked-back hair was ailing at the top, and I felt sure the large mustache covering his mouth was grown as compensation. The way he held himself spoke of money, but I felt sure he lacked manners. I had seen many men like him and always stayed well away.

He was of the kind that only wanted one thing of any woman. I felt sure that his kind only saw women as possetions and nothing more. I could only hope that Ashan wasn't like that as he also came from money.

The client's deep voice was a huge contrast to his companion's shrill one. The companion's stocky appearance and bushy red hair didn't suit his voice at all. Yet, he didn't give off the same vibe as the client. He was a man not born in the business but most likely a bookkeeper or something of the kind.

The client was a real hands-on creep, I thought as I turned, holding out the tray for Ashan. I couldn't help but notice the client or his companion smelled of old booze and cheap cigars. The stench tickled my nose, and I had to hold back a sneeze.

As Ashan reached for a glass, I pulled up my nose. He caught my drift and shook his head at me. Wiggling my nose, I straightened up, ready to return the tray to the bar. But as I was about to walk out, I felt a pat on my ass.

Swinging around to the client in anger, I dropped the tray to the small table and was about to slap him in the face. No man has the right to grab at me. But before my hand was fully in the air, Ashan had risen and pulled me onto his lap.

"Come sit with me for a minute," he added as he pulled my arm down as well.

I was surprised by his action but appreciated it. Feeling his firm grip on my hips, I shifted slightly as he moved me more onto one leg. It felt a little awkward but comforting at the same time. He was protective, and I was glad about it. Yet, he should have scolded the client. I had half a mind to do so myself but bit down on my lower lip to prevent making a scene.

The client was saying something about a missing associate when I initially entered the booth. But now everyone's attention seemed to be on me. The client's smile spread from ear to ear as he stared at me with googly eyes. For a moment, I felt dirty and exposed. I wanted nothing but to get back to the suite and change into my usual clothes.

This scene wasn't for me I realized. I wouldn't have made a good spy as my temper was slightly edgy I thought.

I tried standing, but Ashan's grip on my hips was firm. He held me down tightly as I tried to squirm out of his grip. I knew he needed this deal, but I wasn't comfortable with the client gawking at me like I was about to become his next meal.

Ashan spoke over my shoulder. "We'll, I truly do not know." He said in a charming tone. Glancing at him, I was shocked by the warm smile he offered the client. Even his eyes were soft and friendly as he continued. "As I said earlier, he abruptly left after receiving a call. I have not heard from him since. I think he was going to meet up with someone else."

His unexpected charismatic behavior threw me off guard as my mind was suddenly distracted by all of him. Before my eyes, Ashan turned into a smooth talker. Honey seemed to flow out of his mouth as he spoke. Having his sexy voice in my ear caused heat to rush through me.

Suddenly, I couldn't help but notice his firm chest and strong arms as he gripped my hips. He smelled good, a fresh, minty odor that traveled over my shoulder as he spoke to the client. I was so distracted I couldn't even hear what the man was saying anymore as my mind traveled back to the room.

Turning to the client, I caught his eyes still on me. Then I felt Ashan's hand gripping me tightly around my waist while his other hand traveled from my knee a little up my thigh. My body tingled as he shifted me from his leg more solidly onto him.

He raised his hand and softly moved my hair out of my neck as he spoke. Feeling his hot breath passing my neck sent shivers down my spine. His hand, which now lay on my shoulder, slowly caressed my arm as he moved it back down to my waist. The client's eyes grew wider with each move.

I felt sure he was enjoying the show as he licked his puffy lips. His eyes seemed to water as he shifted forward on the couch. I didn't appreciate the way his appetite seemingly grew with each move I made. Closing my eyes for a split second, I wished I had never agreed to this meeting.

Wiggling lightly on Ashan's lap, trying to loosen his grip, I felt his hard dick pumping under me. Leaning a sliver forward and opening my legs a couple of inches, I could feel his stiffness much better. My heart was racing, and it was difficult to control my breathing as Ashan's hands moved up and down my thighs.

The room unexpectedly heated up, and it felt like I was in a sauna. Suddenly, Ashan gripped both my hips with force as he spoke to the client, leaning slightly to my side. I was sure he was trying to hold me still, but it was hard not to move as my body appeared to have a mind of its own. My hands felt sticky from the sweat forming in them, and my lungs felt like they were about to stop working as I struggled to find air to fill them.

Leaning back on his lap, feeling my body filling with desire, I saw the client gawking at me. "How about sharing the little lady with me?" The client said softly. I almost thought I had heard wrong until Ashan growled back at him.

"She's off-limits, not available," Ashan barked at the client. I was shocked at his abruptness after just hearing him smooth-talk the client. I could see the client's companion was also taken aback by it. Yet, the client still appeared calm.

"I want to do business with you," the man said; his grin made me shudder, and not in a good way.

Glancing at Ashan, I felt sure he noticed it, too. His face looked like it was growing in size as he started to turn red. I didn't know him too well, but I had seen this look on many men before. Ashan was about to explode.

I realized that this meeting was about to turn into a boxing match just looking at Ashan's face. I had to push down the disgust I felt at the client and the lust I felt for Ashan to safe the deal.

CHAPTER 10 - ASHAN

Her squirming had caused all my senses to light up. I needed this meeting to be over. "You know what," I spoke out in a low voice. I tried my best to keep Jamie on my lap, but it wasn't working too well. "How about you think about it and let me know when you're ready. Sound good to you."

"Yes, yes," the client said, moving to the edge of his seat. "But you could sweeten the deal by including her, you know."

The words had barely left his mouth before I felt my body tense up. My grip on her hips tightened as my mouth pulled up. I was about to explode.

"Did you not hear me the first time?" I breathed out between clenched teeth. "I said she was not available."

The shit was about to hit the fan. Jamie placed her hands firmly on mine and squeezed them as she leaned forward again. If she only knew how it drove me insane every time she moved.

"But, sir," she breathed out in a sensual tone. "You want to take all the excitement of the hunt out of the game."

The client gave her a creepy smile. Keeping my composure, I shifted my position. "Sir, I suggest you consider the deal first, and maybe later, we could meet up for a drink," Jamie added.

He sat back, looking very chuffed with himself. I tried to push Jamie aside to get to the client. He had no right to her; she was mine. Glancing over her shoulder, Jamie gave me a warning look and shook her head. Now she was reprimanding me?

"Well then, little miss," he said, standing up. "Ashan, I will contact you shortly to sort the details. You can count on that," he added, looking over her at me before ushering his companion out.

As the man and his stocky companion left, I felt like a beehive. Yet, she saved the deal, and I had to give her it. She was mine, and she ought to know that. How could she flirt so openly with that, that...

I didn't even know what to call him. He was no man, that was for sure. Watching him made me sick. I felt my temper calming slightly as my feelings toward her took over. She was mine, and I wasn't about to share her. But I was about to drag her back upstairs.

Suddenly, the lights dimmed out. Jamie didn't move, she sat quietly as staff and customers moved around just outside the booth. Still stiff from her earlier stirring on my lap, I slowly moved my hand up her thigh.

Jamie parted her legs as I pushed further up. My fingers were on fire by the time I reached her pussy. I was shocked to discover she wasn't wearing any underwear. As my fingers slipped between her pussy lips, I felt an intense heat accompanied by a lot of moisture.

She was wet and wiggling as my fingers slipped into her. My dick throbbed harder as she leaned back into me. Her breathing was jagged and quick. There was no point in prolonging this anymore. I had to have her before I lost all control.

Pulling my hand out, I grabbed her wrist as I pushed Jamie to her feet. She staggered slightly as I moved out of the booth, pulling her with me. We seamlessly walked through the course of people and tables as the lights came on and went off a couple more times. By the time we reached the stairs, the power had been restored. One less thing, I had to focus on.

Heading up the stairs to the suite, I felt my heart racing. Except for my need to be with her, I also had to clarify some things. As we entered the suite, I flung her around into my arms. Staring deeply into her eyes, I had to say my piece before I drowned in them.

"Jamie," I breathed out, trying hard to control my hunger for her. "Never do that again. You are mine. Do you understand?"

She nodded and was about to reply, but I couldn't wait. As her lips parted, I pulled her in tighter and covered her mouth with mine. She tasted sweeter than wine. My mind whirled with the intensity of her kiss.

I tried to control my shaking hands as I pulled the zipper of her dress down. Jamie fumbled at my shirt buttons. Her soft touch drove me wild. Slipping the dress off her shoulders, I kissed her neck.

Her hands froze on my chest as she lifted her head and let out a moan. Shoving the dress to the floor, I lifted her into my arms and moved across the room. As I lifted her, Jamie flung her arms around my neck, and her legs wrapped around my waist.

She was panting as I nibbled at her neck. Feeling the edge of the bed against my calves, I took hold of her sides and flung her to the bed. Moving at lightning speed, I rid myself of my pants. My dick sprung up out of its confines, ready for action.

Looking at her spread out on the bed before me fueled my flames. As I got onto the bed. Crawling up from her feet, I growled softly. Jamie giggled as she pushed herself up onto her elbows. Her laughter sounded like music to my ears.

As I moved, I pushed her legs apart, laying soft bites as I went. Jamie wiggled under my touch but didn't object. Pushing up between her legs, I tasted her sweet essence. Jamie collapsed back on the bed, her moans filling the air as I licked her pussy.

Her skin was like velvet as I continued up. She was warm and smooth under me. As I hovered above her, Jamie placed her hands on my cheeks and moved them into my hair. She pulled me in, kissing me back hard. As sparks flew between us, I lowered myself between her legs.

I felt her pussy throbbing as I pushed my dick deep into her. I moved in and out twice, slowly and softly. Then, I pushed hard and fast a couple of times. Jamie gasped as I moved.

She pulled her legs to my sides as I moved. Lifting myself slightly, I took hold of her legs, bringing them further up. Jamie's moans turned to pants as I moved faster and harder.

She dug her nails into my back, and I felt her explode. I slowed down as I came with her, struggling to catch my breath as my lungs burned; I couldn't help but smile down at her.

It was quick and fierce but satisfying. Rolling onto the bed next to her, I stared at the ceiling. "Jamie," I whispered as she rose from the bed. She entered the bathroom and closed the door without a word. I let her go, not sure what to do about her actions. I knew she enjoyed it as much as I did, and that was clear from her scratching and moaning.

Well, I felt sure she did if I had to judge by her dazzled look and beaming smile. I was hesitant about her sudden disappearance, though, but I decided to catch up on some work and give her some space. Getting dressed, I headed to my office and left the door unlocked.

If she wanted to talk, she'd come find me.

Chapter 11 - Jamie

I just stood for a bit, opened the taps, and allowed the water to run its course. Still in shock, I stared up at the ceiling. The sex, even though it was hard and rough, was amazing. I had never experienced anything like it before, and he entranced me.

I smiled as my hands moved over my body, remembering his touch. Closing my eyes, I moved my hands down over my breasts, across my stomach, and onto my hips. My skin still tingled from the excitement.

Lathering myself in soap, I noticed tiny spots on my inner thighs where he had nibbled. They didn't hurt and would be gone by tomorrow. But washing over them sent vibrations through me as my mind recalled the intensity of each one. How could any man cause such turmoil within, I wondered as my stomach made knots.

Stepping out and wrapping the fluffy robe around me, I heard the suite door opening and shutting. Brushing out my hair, I wondered where Ashan was going or if someone had entered. Entering the suite, I found it was empty. I sat on the edge of the bed for a bit, still in awe of our intense sex.

There was a knock at the door. I was sure it wouldn't be Ashan. I couldn't see him knocking, but one never knew. Opening the door, I was delightfully surprised to find it was one of the women who had brought me the food and clothing the previous day.

At least it wasn't Ana; I would have sent her away if it had been. Even though I had only met her twice, she was incredibly mean, and I felt wary around her. I opened the door wider as this woman brought up a tray with coffee and food. As the delicious aroma filled the air, I was suddenly starving. "Please, come in," I said, holding the door open for her. She quietly pushed the trolley in and looked from me to the mess, grinning.

Only then, noting the state of the suite, I blushed. I could only imagine what she was thinking. "Sorry for the mess, don't let it bother you," I added, taking a deep breath. "Please sit with me for a bit if you can. Oh, and I'm Jamie," I finished, holding out my hand.

"I'm Cleo," she replied, shaking my hand. "You need some help sorting things out?"

"Thanks, Cleo, that would be great but let's have some coffee first?" I responded as I lifted the pot from the tray. Cleo nodded as she started picking up the clothing which I had thrown around earlier.

She sat with me while we drank our coffee, and I questioned her about the staff and routines, learning more about the den. Once we were done, she assisted me in moving and packing away the clothing, jewelry, and makeup. With everything in place, the suite looked functional again.

Cleo stayed and sat with me until I had finished eating before saying goodnight and leaving with the empty tray.

Laying back on the bed, I reminisced for a bit, still blown away by how good the sex was. I wondered if Ashan would be coming to bed tonight and didn't mind if he decided to. But when I woke in the early morning hours, the bed next to me was still empty.

Staring up at the ceiling, I told myself it was for the best. After all, I wasn't planning on staying too long. Once I found Ben's real identity, I could clear my name and get out of this unfortunate situation. So, what if I had to sleep with Ashan a couple of times? He was extremely handsome, and the sex was out of this world. It wasn't the worst fate, at least it wasn't Pedro.

After rolling around for about half an hour, I decided to get up. I couldn't sleep further, so I showered and dressed. Back in the suite, I sat on the chaise and flipped through the stations. I could find nothing I wanted to watch, so I turned the TV off.

Remembering that Ashan had left all the doors unlocked so I wouldn't feel trapped again, I decided to have a look around. I was roaming through the halls and rooms when the staff started arriving.

Bored out of my mind with still no access to hacking tools, I struck up conversations with everyone I passed.

With no phone, computer, or even a radio, I befriended the den workers. I did try the TV and listening device in the small room, but they had limited access. Talking to the server women and even Ashan's bodyguards gave me a little insight into how things worked around here.

The more I learned about him. However small or little the information was, the more Ashan intrigued me. I made some friends as the days passed. Except for Ana, it seemed that she treated everyone nastily. It wasn't only me; she had a temper but appeared to hate all people equally.

I also learned more about all the den had to offer during my first week. Ashan had built up an impressive empire. Walking through the entertainment areas, I wondered where he would go if he sold the place. After all, it was also his home, and it was not just a business as Ashan was staying here. Remembering he didn't come to bed all week, I considered other places where he may have spent his nights. I wondered if he had another home somewhere in the city and if he would show me someday.

Moving back down to the restaurant, I ordered some breakfast directly from the kitchen. They had a special muffin and croissant breakfast Cleo insisted I try but only on Fridays. Placing my order with one of the waiters, I saw Ana was also there. She was fighting with some of the kitchen staff. Watching her, I wondered what her role here actually was. She was very bossy and cruel to most of the staff. Whenever I noticed her, she would shout orders, yet I couldn't see Ashan employing someone like her as a manager.

Ana stormed up to me as I was about to leave the kitchen and find a table in the dining area. "You know you don't belong here, princess. You're nothing but a bargaining chip," she spat at me with her hands on her hips. This comment was out of place and unasked for. Feeling my anger rising, I shook my head, pushing it back down.

"And what exactly is your role?" I asked calmly.

Ana looked me up and down, then made a 'puff' sound before storming past me, shoving me backward as she went. I didn't appreciate the way she constantly undermined me. I thought she was saddened by the fact that Ashan married me. Even if my marriage to Ashan was for other reasons than love, he chose me. He could have married her, but he didn't, and there had to be a reason for that.

I sat down and had breakfast alone as the cleaners and waiters scurried around, preparing the place for opening. I found the muffins delightful, and the croissants were simply out of this world. Afterward, I headed to the kitchen. I just had to get the recipe and learn how to make them. The chef agreed to teach me if I joined him in the kitchen at 4 in the morning. Excited to learn how to cook while I stayed here, I explored some more.

For the rest of the morning, I avoided any area Ana was in. I roamed around and chatted with some of the other staff as I moved up to the pool area. The previous day, I had spent some time in the jacuzzi but today was going to be a scorcher with the sun already heating the world outside. After several laps in the pool, I returned to the suite.

The rest of the day went pretty much the same as the previous ones and once again, I slept alone. The next morning, I wondered why Ashan was not returning to his suite, I mean really, it's been a week. Was the business so demanding, or was he ignoring me? Even though I could now go anywhere within the den, I still couldn't leave, and not even seeing a glimpse of him for the last couple of days made me nervous.

Proceeding down to the kitchen, I decided that after breakfast, I would look for him and find out what was happening. I needed access to more than clothes, meals, and TV. I necessitated my kind of entertainment as well. Plus, I still had to find Ben, and access to the net was imperative.

Today's breakfast consisted of sausages, eggs, and toast with a bowl of fruit. It was tasty, but Cleo was right, the muffins and croissants were better. Heading back to the suite, I looked for Ashan, but there was still no sign that he had been back.

I decided to wait for a while, hoping he might be up for lunch. I had left a message in his office and told the guards I was looking for him, so he had to show up sometime. Switching on the TV, I searched for something to watch. I had seen most of the movies that were showing and there was little else interesting, so I turned it off again. I had never been a fan of sitting around doing nothing.

To me, watching hours and hours of soaps or other similar programs was just that. A waste of my time. After I had lunch alone again, I decided to go look for Ashan as he still did not show up. I started at his office, but he wasn't there. The note I left was on his table where I had placed it; he hadn't been back since morning. So, I asked the staff if they'd seen him, as it was odd that he hadn't even been back to his office all morning.

Going from floor to floor and room to room, no one knew where he was. I checked the dining hall, the kitchen, the bar area, the booths, and the gambling floor but couldn't find him. Entering the last floor, I felt sure he would be in one of the entertainment area rooms as there was nowhere else to go.

He had to be here somewhere. If not, then he would have left the gambling den without a word, and that would not be acceptable. He could come and go as he pleased, but leaving me alone all day and night was just bad manners. I was considered to be his wife. Even if it wasn't real for either of us, there was surely supposed to be communication and sharing.

Walking from room to room, I opened each door and glanced in. Some of the rooms were decorated blue, others were gold, and there was a silver room. All of them had a variety of seating and tables, some had stages and poles, and others had what looked like massage beds or something similar.

I wondered what could happen in these rooms, but I felt sure I was seeing things that didn't happen. There was no reason to knock as it was still early, and no clients had entered the den yet. Most of the rooms were either empty or had cleaning staff in.

As I moved from one room to the next, I felt hollow in my gut. Something was off, but I didn't know what. Only eight rooms were on this floor, and I had already gone through five. Only three were left; if he wasn't here, I would sneak into his office and scour through his computer. The thought of him walking in on me while I was on his computer made me grin; it would be kind of funny. Yet, I was sure he would go off the deep side.

As I opened the sixth door, I caught a whiff of perfume as it streamed out through the door. Popping my head around the door, I stopped and pushed it all the way open. This wasn't what I ever imagined I would find. The picture before me flashed through my mind, and I had to blink just to make sure I was seeing it correctly.

It looked like a room set up for private shows. It wasn't huge and could maybe fit four or five people. In the middle was a small stage with a glowing pink pole down the middle of it. It was lit up by six small lights pouring a soft pink light down and out toward the chairs. On one side of the stage were three single couches. They looked puffy and actually very comfortable.

On the other side were two chaise lounges like the ones in Ashan's suite. The perfume I smelled belonged to Ana, who was in the room. But she wasn't alone; she was with Ashan. Ana turned and glared at me. Her eyes were filled with hate, but her grin portrayed an evil satisfaction and a sinfulness I had never seen in anyone before.

She was wearing a silky white see-through gown with no undergarments, as her ass was clearly visible. Her large breasts hung out the front as she stood, turning halfway towards me. Behind her on the floor lay a coat I suspected she wore over the skimpy gown. On the couch before her sat Ashan.

Ana had her one foot on his chest as she stood naked before him. The black high heels she wore pressed into his firm chest and for a second, I wondered if he liked painful foreplay. Her other foot was between his legs on the floor. Ashan was holding the leg against him, but it didn't appear as if he was pushing it away. His eyes grew wide with shock when he saw me, a sure sign he didn't expect me to find them.

Unexpectedly, I felt hurt and jealous. Breathing in deeply, I felt my heart being ripped from my chest. I was suddenly hot, sweaty, and feeling very ill. Blinking, I tried to stop the sudden onset of tears bombarding my eyes. I could only hope Ashan hadn't noticed my pain as I retreated and slammed the door shut. Leaning against it for a second, still holding the handle, I breathed quickly and deeply, hoping to fill my shrinking lungs.

I was sure I had made myself clear when I told him I wouldn't be with him if she was still in the picture. Shutting my eyes and squeezing them, I wished it was all in my mind. Glancing around, the walls appeared to be closing in on me as my vision blurred. They were still hooking up my mind screamed at me as the image replayed before my eyes repeatedly.

No, no, I told myself as I ran down the stairs. My legs felt weak, and my breathing shallow. Taking two steps at a time, I almost tumbled over.

My mind was competing with my heart to a finish line that didn't exist as I tried to push the reality out. Stopping in front of the suite door, I wasn't sure if I should stay or run. I felt a darkness pushing up as rage filled every inch of my being.

How could I have been so stupid and careless? Men like him don't change. They may look normal and decent, but they clearly weren't. I had to decide, and I would have to do it quickly. Stay or go, I asked myself as I opened the suite door and walked in.

Chapter 12 - Ashan

After one of the most incredible nights, I've ever had, I thought some space would do us both some good. I spent the next couple of nights in my office on the couch as the sex was unbelievable, and my mind was struggling to focus on anything except her. Somehow, Jamie had bewitched me, I was sure of it. My heart and mind couldn't let go, and this wasn't normal. No woman has ever occupied my mind, never mind my heart.

Yet somehow, she did, and I couldn't let go. Everything I tried to do, my mind persistently went to her everywhere I turned. She was just another woman, nothing special, I told myself. With enough time and space, I felt sure things would return to normal. But moving through my daily routine had become mechanical the last couple of days.

My mind and body functioned separately after all these years. It was like the one no longer needed the other. Plus, most of the staff knew their duties, which I was glad for. I only checked in and assisted if there was an issue. Going about my usual routine was harder than it normally was.

I was preoccupied and only wanted to go back to my suite and spend the day in bed with Jamie. Eventually, I would have to face her, and I knew she would come looking. But maybe I could wait another day or two. The struggle was real and seeing her could make it more complicated. In the kitchen, I grabbed some coffee and stood in the back, watching the hustle as everyone moved in and out.

Hearing Ana entering the kitchen and booming at the servers, I moved into the shadows. I didn't want to confront her, and soon I would have to decide if she would stay or leave. Then I saw Jamie entering, and I moved even further back. She ordered breakfast then, seemingly, had words with Ana, who stormed out shoving her back. I stood silently watching in disbelief.

Jamie and Ana were two worlds colliding, they were nothing alike. Ana always took charge and spat out orders like a drill sergeant. Jamie on the other hand was soft and listened when people spoke to her. Ana had become worse over the years, she used to be a lot softer, but she always got things done. However, lately, I have noticed her becoming more aggressive and possessive, which I didn't like.

I felt like a stalker hiding in the shadows, but Jamie fascinated me. Plus, I wasn't ready to show my feelings, and my body would betray me if I spoke to her now. Heck, I wasn't sure what was happening to me. But Jamie was driving me wild, and I needed to know why. So, I decided to follow her for a bit.

Jamie spent most of her morning exploring and getting to know the staff, as I heard she had done the previous day as well, and the ones before it. As she headed for a swim, I went to my office, made some calls and dealt with machine issues for the rest of the day.

It was early morning when I was called to the second floor again. Most of the morning went routine after that. Returning to my office shortly after lunchtime, I saw a note Jamie had left and thought I would catch-up with her as soon as I was done. I was about halfway through my emails when one of the guards came to call me.

There was a knock at the door. "Boss, sorry, Ana sent me," Claus said, entering my office. Glancing up, his expression was that of someone who had just received a scolding or bad news. I suspected it was a scolding, seeing that Ana had sent him. At some point, I would have to stop her aggression towards the staff. "Miss Ana told me to let you know studio six has some kind of issue."

Glancing up from my laptop, I felt a bit irritated at Ana. "What's the issue, my man?" I inquired calmly, as it wasn't his fault he had to call me away.

He seemed overly nervous, tripling around like a little girl as he continued. "Not sure boss; she only told me to call you and put a rush on it. Her face and hair were all done up though." Claus glanced down at the floor as he spoke the last bit.

Knowing Ana, I was sure it was minor, but I nodded and rose. The guard walked ahead of me to the third floor and then left. Heading to room six, I wondered what Ana was up to now and what kind of issue could there be if she had put on make-up.

Pushing the door open, I noticed the room was dark with all the lights off. "Ana," I said about to leave again, seeing that she wasn't there. Yet, she had been as I could smell her perfume. As I started pulling the door closed, I heard a movement.

"Have a seat, hun," I heard her reply faintly from somewhere within. Glancing back in, one of the lights came on, making only enough glow for me to see one of the couches.

Moving in, I felt irritated at her. "Ana, I don't have time for this. What's the issue in here?" I asked, looking for her. Feeling her grab my rear end, I spun around. "Ana, stop," I said as she shoved me backward.

Falling back, I felt the chair encasing me as the other lights in the room came on. Before me stood Ana with basically nothing on except for a see-through gown and stilettoes. "Ana, this has to stop," I said, taking hold of the armrests to pull myself up. What would Jamie think if she saw this my mind screamed.

"No, no, no," Ana replied, pushing me back with one foot on my chest and waving a finger in the air. "We're not done, hun; we're just getting started. Relax and let me remind you," she added, leaning forward.

Grabbing hold of her calf to prevent the heel of her shoe from entering my chest, I heard the door opening behind her. Glancing around her, I saw Jamie standing at the door. The look on her face as she saw us affected me more than I was prepared for. I knew very well what it must have looked like. In her mind, after not being with her or seeing her for a couple of days, this must have confirmed some kind of idea she had.

She had explicitly told me Ana should no longer be in the picture if I wanted a future with her. I didn't want to hurt her, and this wasn't my doing, but I didn't know if she would believe me now. Seeing the tears in her eyes and the shock on her face as she stepped back out stung. My gut tightened, and my heart pounded in my chest. Feeling my guilt driving my anger, I knew this had to stop.

Ana was out of control, I pushed Ana back and rose quickly. She staggered backward but steadied herself against the pole. Leaning around it, she softly spoke. "Ashan baby, so much fire always between us; I love your passion."

Boiling from anger, I raised my voice as I replied. "Ana, stop, it's over. There is no more me and you. Don't ever try this again."

Hanging on the pole she smiled at me and spoke, "Hunny, baby, you don't mean that; you know we have more than a mere fire. Plus, I can give you what she can't."

I was astounded that Ana was still pushing this. How was the anger in my voice and my words not enough for her to understand? Staring at her, I realized this was never going to end as she seemed to only hear what she wanted. I knew I would have to stop this madness once and for all.

"Ana," I breathed out, trying to stay calm. My hands formed fists, which I kept tightly against my sides. She was still a woman, and I wasn't ever going to hit a woman no matter how angry I was. "It is time for you to pack up and leave, Ana, you have overstayed your welcome." I walked to the door and waved my guards closer. "Claus will escort you out. Please, leave."

Looking back at her as she picked up her coat, Ana was stunned. She started shaking her head as I stepped out of the room and gave the guards instructions. "Please see she gets her things and escort her off the premises," Claus shook his head in agreement. "If she gives you any trouble just let me know."

Ana walked slowly out of the room, seemingly defeated. Maybe now she realized that I meant what I said. "Goodbye, Ana," I uttered before heading down to find Jamie. I knew it looked bad, but I was sure once Jamie knew what had happened, she would understand. She had to, I thought as I ran to the suite.

As I moved, my mind spun. A headache was developing somewhere in the back and would soon be pounding at my skull. But I had to make things right with Jamie. My heart raced as I walked toward the suite door. I had never felt this way about any woman before. As I went, I tried to formulate my thoughts and organize my words as I needed to explain what she saw with care.

Before I could reach the suite, Leo and Luder stopped me. "Ashan," Leo said, blocking me in the hallway. He sounded and looked upset. Glancing at them, I noticed that Luder looked kind of disappointed.

"Hey, guys," I replied quickly, unsure what was going on, but I needed to get to Jamie. "Now's not a good time. I'm a bit busy and in a rush."

"No," Luder said, raising his voice slightly as he stepped in before me and grabbed me by the shoulder. He held my arm as he turned me to face him. "You need to explain first. We are family, and there are some things we don't hide or do in secret; you know that!"

I only wanted to get to the suite and Jamie, but I could see they were seriously upset. "You got married and didn't let anyone know?" Leo spat as he joined Luder before me.

The walls rapidly felt like they were closing in. Sweat broke out on the back of my neck, I knew this was bound to happen at some point. But how did they find out now at this moment, I wondered. Yet, discussing it now wasn't the right time, not with all that had just happened. If I didn't hurry, Jamie would leave. I had to explain to her that what she saw wasn't real, or the whole picture for that matter.

"Is this true?" Luder asked, raising his eyebrows. I could see my brother felt hurt even though he tried to hide it behind his anger. "Ashan, explain yourself." He added in an abrupt tone.

"I knew this would come guys, but really not know," I pleaded, hoping to get Jamie settled before telling them. "Please, guys, I'll explain everything. Just not now, I really have to go. Can we do this tomorrow?" I continued. I felt like a jumping jack and had to fight the urge to just run to the suite.

"What else could be more important?" Leo snapped at me as I pushed through them. Luder tried pulling me back, but I kept moving, turning out of his grasp.

Glancing back as I went forward, I replied over my shoulder. "Please, tomorrow, guys. I promise we will sit down and talk about everything."

I stormed forward to the suite, leaving them standing there. It did look like Luder wanted to come after me, but Leo pulled him back. A couple of seconds later, I entered the suite. It was empty. I searched all the rooms but didn't find her, Jamie was gone. Checking her wardrobe, I noticed her old clothing was missing, but nothing else.

Rushing out, I searched the entire den floor by floor, and room by room. I was relieved that Leo and Luder had seemingly left, and I didn't run into them during my search. I spoke to the guards and other staff. No one had seen her. Would Jamie leave the den, did I make her go out there where her life was in imminent danger?

For a moment, my heart stopped as my chest tightened. I struggled to catch my breath as my mind played through all the scenarios of what could happen. She was out there and not safe. My legs felt wobbly and weak, I had to find her.

Gathering my guards, I asked them to search the territory. We had to move quickly and do it thoroughly. If Jamie went outside our borders, who knew what would happen? I sent out a photo to all the guards and told them to let me know if she was spotted. After taking a stiff drink, I also went out, driving up and down the streets in search of her.

CHAPTER 13 - JAMIE

How could I even consider staying? No, I had to leave. Who did he think he was? After changing back into my clothes, I sneaked out of the den. I moved slowly and cautiously down the stairs, bundling between the clients as they started filling the den. I could not get caught leaving. He would come up with all kinds of excuses, but I knew what I saw, and there was no hiding it.

My heart felt heavy, but I couldn't allow my feelings to get the upper hand. Departing from the den, I moved cautiously through the large parking area. I stayed between the cars as I proceeded to the gate. Where there were no cars, I stayed close to the outer walls, moving in behind the dumpsters just inside the main gate. I watched as four guards came by.

They were glancing around, and I felt sure they were already searching for me. Thinking they had all passed, I ran for the exit. It was only a short distance, but as I stepped into the street, I heard someone calling out behind me. Looking back, I felt my blood turn to ice as one of the guards came charging at me. The others weren't far behind him.

I just turned and ran with no clear direction or idea of where to go. A couple of blocks away was a park. I ran in and hid in the shadows of a small bridge. The guards passed twice before heading back towards the den. Positive that this time they had left, I quickly moved out of the Morozov territory.

I still had no idea where to go or who to contact; I was alone and felt defeated. I was surveying the area as I went and knew I needed to find somewhere where I would be safe and lay low. Tired and sore from running once again, I decided to enter a bar. It was quiet, with little to no people inside. The place looked normal enough not to be Bratva, and it appeared decent.

I was reasonably sure it would be safe. In one corner was a group of about five playing pool and minding their own business. They didn't even notice me as I moved in. There was a couple in another corner close to the jukebox kissing and another pair at a table chatting up a storm. Taking a seat, I ordered a drink and watched the people from my corner of the bar.

The lights in the corner where I sat weren't as bright as the rest of the room. It gave me some cover, I thought, sipping my drink. I knew I would have to figure something out as I couldn't stay here. With my current situation, I wouldn't be able to stay in one place for too long.

Breathing in deeply, I closed my eyes, trying to regain my senses. Yet, closing my eyes wasn't such a good idea after all. I saw Ana standing over Ashan and that stupid smirk on her face. I should have slapped her, I thought. But no, what did I do? I ran like a child after the playground bully had shoved her.

"Hi, there." Startled out of my thoughts by the voice behind me, I swung around so quickly that I almost toppled off the bar stool. "Sorry, I didn't mean to scare you," the petite woman standing slightly behind me said. Her voice was soft and kind, but I had to listen carefully to hear her through the noise.

Lifting one hand at her, I replied. "It's okay, I was just thinking. Can I help you?"

She was small, seemingly no threat to me. Her chestnut eyes appeared a bit too large for her face, as did her wide smile, exposing her abnormally large teeth. She was dressed in tight blue jeans and a loose red hoodie. The hoodie was pulled up like mine as if she was hiding from life, and I felt a pull to her. It could have been her nonthreatening appearance or the similarities my mind made.

I wasn't sure why, but I instantly felt a strange bond with her. "May I sit with you?" she asked, glancing around. I nodded as I turned back to the bar. "I'm Bea," she added, sliding onto the stool next to me. "I haven't seen you here before."

My mind was still swirling with all that had happened, and my guard was down. My mood was in the dumps, and I thought a little company may just be what I needed. "Jamie," I replied, staring into my drink, wishing I could disappear into the glass.

"You look tired. Have you eaten? Would you like a meal?" Bea said, hailing the bartender. Glancing up into the mirror behind the bar, I saw my reflection. It did look like I was something the cat dragged in. My tattered clothing and, once again, I had dirt on my face as if I had slept on the curb. It must have come from hiding under the bridge, I thought.

She ordered a plate of chips and another round of drinks for us. I felt thankful and hoped she didn't ask too many questions. Our conversation started out small, but I thought she shared openly with me. She told me about her small apartment a couple of blocks away and growing up with two brothers.

I wished I knew what having a family and being loved was like. The more she shared, the more I longed for a normal life. As she spoke, I reconsidered my actions. I had never had anyone, and Ashan offered me a somewhat normal life. Maybe I could have overlooked Ashan's indiscretions. At least I would have still had something I considered.

After she ordered another round of drinks, I started feeling uncomfortable. Her questions became more specific as time passed, and this sent up a red flag. Once I took note of the direction her questions started hinting at and studied the patrons around us more closely, some more red flags started popping up.

Realizing I had walked into a trap, I knew that my next moves would have a strong impact on whether I got out or got captured. Bea and about a third of the people around me were surely part of the enemies. I was astounded that they had still been tracking or watching out for me. I was so intent on getting away from Ashan that I hadn't even thought of my reason for being with him.

It's not been months, but it has been a week since I ended up married and staying with Ashan. I felt sure I would have had some time to make a plan. Now, here I was, feeling like a cornered wolf. My heart pounded at my ribcage, and the blood in my veins turned to ice as I unexpectedly felt dizzy. I breathed in slowly and deeply, trying not to panic or show fear.

Glancing at Bea, I spoke in an even tone as I breathed out with care. "Excuse me, I have to go to the bathroom. A little too much liquid, I think."

Bea smiled at me as I slid off the stool. I hoped she hadn't picked up on my fear. Walking to the bathroom, I kept my head low, pulling my hoodie over my face. Yet, I made sure to check if anyone was following my movements. There were at least six men that I could pick up on.

Closing the bathroom door behind me, I locked it and quickly sought a way out. Scanning the window, I felt sure I would fit; it might be tight, but I would go through it. Standing on the toilet seat lid, I opened the small square window and glanced outside.

The immediate area was quiet. I pushed myself up and stepped on the toilet bowl to get some more height. Forcing myself through the window, I didn't even consider what came next. Dropping to the ground, a moan escaped me as I twisted my arm, trying to block the fall into the brush.

Rushing to my feet, I hoped no one had heard me. Rubbing my arm, I stuck my head through the bushes. To one side, I saw two men with guns coming my way. They weren't in a hurry, so I was sure they hadn't heard me. But I knew it was only a matter of time before Bea would start looking for me. I considered them to just be on their regular rounds, but if I sat still, I might be discovered.

I had no other option as there was nowhere else to hide. I would have to run. My heart now felt as if it was pounding in my throat. Sweat covered my body, and I had not even started running yet. Feeling slightly numb with fear, I knew I had to move; the longer I waited, the closer they got.

Moving against the wall away from them, I crawled, hoping not to be noticed. But I froze as I heard them shuffling through the bushes below the window. My heart was pounding so hard I was sure it could be heard from miles away. Holding my breath, I tried to silence the beating in my mind.

Wanting to make a run for it, I stuck my head out to see if the street was clear. But as soon as I did, I realized I should have sat still.

"There she is," one of the guards screamed, pointing my way.

My life would be over if they caught me. I leaped to my feet and ran as fast as I could. I dared not to look back in fear of seeing them closing in. Or worse, seeing them aiming their guns at me.

About a block down, I ran full speed into a man coming out of another club. We tumbled to the ground and heard the men calling out as they came closer. Scampering to my feet, I saw the man I had run into who caused me to tumble was Pedro.

He held out his hand as he spoke. "Come on, let's get out of here; my cars waiting."

There was no time to think or consider the consequences; I didn't even wonder why he would be in the area. I took his hand, and he pulled me up. His Chevy was idling next to us. I got in and locked the door as he ran around and got in behind the wheel.

Pedro pulled out as the first shots filled the air, and we sped away. Out of breath but not out of danger, as I realized he was the last person on earth I wanted to be close to. I tried to thank him and ask him to stop. But my words wouldn't form properly as I battled to catch my breath.

He drove around up and down streets through different territories for a while before eventually pulling into a dark alley between two warehouses. Now that I was finally calm enough, I spoke. "Thanks, Pedro."

He nodded and gave me a grin as he got out. "I heard you left and was out looking for you. I am glad that I found you when I did, though." He said, opening my door. "Come on, you'll be safe here for now."

Something didn't feel right, and I wanted to leave, but he had just saved my life, and this made it twice now. So, I followed him into one of the warehouses. Maybe I could stay the night and make a plan in the morning I thought glancing around.

Both my lungs and muscles were burning. And I needed rest. I had to clear my mind before moving on. This time, I had to have a plan. I couldn't just go strolling through the street, not knowing who was looking for me. It was clearly not over and too dangerous to be out in the open.

Plus, I knew Pedro a little and felt sure he wasn't a danger. In the back of the warehouse were what appeared to be two makeshift rooms. The rest of the place was empty. One of the rooms had two small windows, and the other a long row of windows.

The one I could see looked like a kitchen and lounge in a single space. Seeing this as we walked closer, I assumed the other one with the smaller window was then his bedroom.

"You live here?" I inquired as he opened the door to the kitchen/lounge area.

Grinning at me again over his shoulder, he responded slowly. "Sometimes, but not always." He held the door open and waved his hand for me to enter. I walked in and looked around. It seemed cozy enough for one person. Maybe I should get a place like this that is off the grid. Smiling at myself, I wondered what Ashan would say about it.

Hearing the door lock behind me, I swung around. "Pedro," I said, feeling fear pushing through me. "What's going on?"

He gave me that grin again as he spoke. "Oh, I'm sure you know. Twice now, I saved you." He licked his lips as he came closer. "You owe me, baby," he blurted out as he grabbed my wrist.

"No, Pedro," I said trying to pull away. "I owe you nothing, let me go."

We turned in circles a couple of times as I struggled to free my hands. After two or three turns, Pedro's posture changed.

He let go of my wrist and grabbed me around my waist as I tried to pass him. Even though I heard the door lock, I wanted to be sure as I saw no other way out except if I jumped through a window. "Jamie, baby girl," he practically shouted as he flung me backward. I tried to stop my fall but only caught the side of the couch.

Falling sideways from it, I hit my head on the small table, falling with me. Before I could get up or move away, Pedro was on top of me. "Girl, you owe me big time, and it's time to pay your dues," he breathed into my neck as he pinned me to the floor.

"No, Pedro, no," I begged, trying to push him off. He was sitting on top of me with my hands pinned above my head.

"If you don't stop struggling, girl, I'll beat ya," He hushed out as I felt one hand move to the buttons of my jeans.

My mind went blank with fear, and I felt paralyzed as I realized he was about to rape me. I started screaming at the top of my voice, hoping to be heard even though I knew we were somewhere secluded.

Even though I was filled with fear, I kept struggling. I wasn't about to allow him to do this to me. I hadn't survived everything to be used like a whore. My fighting spirit wouldn't give up.

CHAPTER 14 - ASHAN

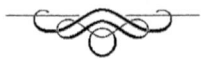

It was getting late, and there was still no sign of her. I was angry and worried at the same time, how could Ana have done that? She knew full well I married Jamie. My men had been out searching the surrounding clubs and parks; they even went to search in the other territories.

There was no sign of her, it was like she had vanished. I couldn't believe she would go so far as to leave our territory, but I didn't want to take any chances. My men knew it had to be done discreetly. We didn't need a war with Jamie still a target and now out there.

A couple of hours passed, I had returned to the den and was on my fourth drink when the call came in. One of my men felt sure he had seen her entering a warehouse on the edge of our territory. After receiving the coordinates, I recognized the location. Pedro was known to hang out there at times. A sense of relief washed over me. If she was with him, she would at least be safe.

I rushed over, wondering why she was with Pedro. Feeling sure that he had just happened to stumble upon her, I was grateful she wasn't out there on the street. I couldn't help but wonder if she was doing okay and why he didn't let me know that he had found her.

Something was wrong. I could feel it in my bones. I had asked my men to wait outside for me, to not enter. I wanted to talk to her calmly and sort things out. I didn't want her to feel like she was being held hostage.

Four of my guards were waiting as instructed when I arrived at the warehouse. They were parked across the street, so I pulled in next to them. I didn't see Pedro's car as I got out, but then again, the place was dark. The warehouse looked quiet and abandoned. "You sure they're here?" I asked as we walked across the road.

Before any of them could answer, we heard the screaming coming from inside. Instantly, my body went cold. There was someone there all right. My guards broke through the door, and we stormed in. The warehouse was dark; the only light came through the windows of the kitchen/lounge area at the back.

Hearing her screams, now clear as day, sent rage through me. Breaking through the door, I saw her on the floor next to the couch. She was kicking and screaming while Pedro sat on top of her with her hands pinned above her head. His one hand was up in the air as if he was about to hit her. He glanced around as we barged in. I saw fear settling on his face as he realized what was happening.

Storming at him, I grabbed him behind the neck, lifting him off her. "You have no right touching my wife," I screamed.

"Ashan, I was going to call," he mumbled as I held him up against the wall.

The last thing I remember doing was flipping him over and smashing him to the ground as I started raining down blows. A deep, dark blackness took over after the first two or three hits.

Somewhere in the distance, I heard Jamie crying and pleading with me to stop. Through the daze of fury, I saw blood splattering the couch and carpet around his head. Feeling his scull cracking with each blow, I knew deep down inside I had to stop but it was like I was no longer in charge. Then I felt big, strong hands taking hold of my arms and pulling me backward.

"Low-life piece of crap," I heard myself saying as I tried to find my feet and push my rage down. "Let me go," I shouted, shaking my head, and pulling at my arms. Looking to my left and then right, I saw Leo and Luder. I forced myself out of the darkness that had taken hold. Leo was on one side holding my arm, and Luder on the other; they wouldn't let go.

"Ashan," Luder said harshly. "You have to calm down, get a grip, man."

Looking down before us on the floor, I saw Pedro. His face was covered in blood, his one eye purple and swollen. He lay there lifeless.

Did I kill him, I wondered as my racing heart started to slow down. The skin on one side of his jaw was torn or ripped, exposing his jawbone, and it appeared he had some hair missing where the white bone of his skull was visible.

There was blood splatter all around him on the carpet and furniture. I shook my head, trying to get a grip on what had happened. Pulling free from Leo and Luder's grip, I staggered back. Two of Leo's guards rushed over and tried to stop the bleeding. Glancing around, I saw Jamie standing by the door with one of my guards. She was sobbing terribly into her hands.

Standing there, I stared at my blood-covered hands. How could I have been so insensitive, how could I lose control like that? This wasn't like me. Luder tapped me on the shoulder as he handed me a cloth and lightly pushed me toward the door. "I think you should move out, brother," he said.

Walking to the door, I reached out for Jamie, but she pulled back from me and walked out before me. Leaving the room, I heard Leo on the phone asking for a clean-up. I watched Jamie walking ahead with Frank; everything still felt like a bad dream. I shook my head but couldn't clear it.

Luder came up behind me, making me jump as he spoke. "Let's go," Still dazed, I went with Luder, following Jamie and my guards as they exited the warehouse. We drove back to the den in silence. The guards took Jamie up to the suite while Luder and I went to my office. Once my hands were washed, I ordered a strong pot of coffee as we waited for Leo.

Standing by the window, I tried to make sense of what happened. Turning, I looked Luder in the eye as I spoke. "I, I, don't know what I thought, I don't know," but Luder interrupted me before I could complete my sentence.

"You weren't thinking, were you?" he said sternly. "You always taunted me for making rash choices, but this, this is messed up."

I turned back to face the window and the world outside. "He was going to rape her," I uttered, still a little shaken up. "I had to stop him, you understand,"

"Even so, Ashan, you know he doesn't only work for us," Luder shot back at me. "You could have handled it better." Luder came to stand beside me. "Killing Pedro will not look good for us. There will be a lot of blowbacks, Ashan."

Hearing the door open, we turned together to see Leo coming in. He didn't look too pleased with me. "What in the name of hell were you thinking? You made a royal mess of things."

I nodded my head. I knew he was right. But hearing her scream, seeing her like that, it drove me blind with anger. "It's just, well, I couldn't just stand there," I responded, even though I knew there was no excuse.

"You could have called us before going there. If your guard didn't let us know, you might have killed him, and then there would have been more than doctor's bills to pay." Leo growled. As they continued to reprimand me, I couldn't focus. My mind was filled with Jamie, and I only wanted to get her out.

Standing here in my office was the last place I wanted to be at that moment. I wanted to leave and check on Jamie. I had to explain to her that what she saw wasn't the real me. She also had to understand that I was trying to protect her. Then I heard Leo saying something about Roman taking care of things, and that I could thank my stars that Pedro wasn't dead.

Shaking my head, I tried to focus on the situation at hand. "So, he's going to be fine then," I said, looking at the two of them.

"Fine," Luder spat at me. "Eventually, but if we were a couple of seconds slower, nothing would have been fine." He pointed a finger at me as he continued. "Do you understand what you have done?"

Leo was furious. I had only seen him like this twice before. I stared blankly at them as my mind kept going back to Jamie. He pinned her and she was kicking and screaming. "I would do it again," I blurted out.

Leo and Luder glanced at each other and back at me. "What?" Leo asked, lifting his hands in the air.

"You heard me. He was sitting on top of her, she was screaming and kicking, he was going to rape her." Taking a deep breath, I turned back to the window before continuing. "If I didn't get there when I did, I don't even want to think what would have happened. He's not worth the trouble." I lowered my head and wished they would just leave so I could go to Jamie.

"Let's talk in the morning," I hear Luder respond as if he had heard my thoughts.

Glancing back, I watched as the two of them left my office. After taking a deep breath, I swallowed the last of my coffee, then left my office and headed to the suite. Entering, I paused, holding my breath. The suite was empty, but then I noticed the bathroom door was slightly ajar. Walking closer, I pushed the door slowly open.

There she was, sitting in the corner of the shower with her eyes shut. The water poured over her like rain. She looked delicate and vulnerable; my heart ached seeing her this way. I fought the urge to pick her up and hold her forever, never letting go again.

Walking closer, I swore to protect her no matter what. I would face any consequences for her. Kneeling by the shower door, I spoke softly, "Jamie, are you okay?"

She glanced up at me, "I'll be fine." She replied. Her tone was flat, and the sparkle in her eyes was gone.

"I'm sorry," I added, wishing I could take away her pain. "Is there anything I can do or anything you need?"

Jamie shook her head, but I couldn't just leave her like this. I took my towel robe from its perch and stood before the shower door, holding it up for her. "Can I hold you?" I asked softly.

Jamie looked miserable but stood and closed to the taps. As she stepped towards me, I wrapped it around her and picked her up. I felt her relaxing slightly in my arms as I carried her to the bed. Placing her down on the bed, Jamie rolled to her side and pulled herself into a ball. I sat down next to her, caressing her hair and rubbing her back, she just lay there with her eyes closed.

"Jamie," I whispered. "I'm so sorry." She didn't move. Her lips were pushed out into a pout, and a layer of sadness seemingly covered her like a blanket. Watching her, I realized that I needed to step up and make amends if I wanted us to work. I sat with her until I was sure she was sleeping.

Back in my office, I made arrangements and sorted some things out after I set an appointment with Leo and Luder for first thing in the morning. There was a lot to do, and it was time to get the family involved. They needed to know why things went the way they did so we could discuss moving forward.

Staring out the window, I felt a wave of guilt. I didn't handle things right from the start. I was over-eager and made so many mistakes. But, moving forward I would set it right. We were a big family and supported each other, I should have included them, and I knew things could have gone better.

CHAPTER 15 - JAMIE

Stretching out, I rolled over in the large bed, patting Ashan's side of the bed, but he wasn't there. Opening my eyes and rolling to my back, I stared up at the ceiling. I actually felt better than I expected. I slept like a rock even with everything that happened and was going on. Being back in Ashan's arms made me feel safe, and grateful for him, but I knew we would have to talk at some point.

Too much had happened for us to simply move on, and I wasn't sure how I felt about him beating up Pedro.

I noticed the suite was empty. Ashan was here when I fell asleep, but he wasn't anymore. Would he be back this time or was he going to ignore me again for a week I wondered.

Sitting up, I saw a trolley at the foot of the bed. Moving closer, I studied its content, as there were a couple of things on it. There were three covered plates, a bag, and a large pot of coffee. As I scooted down to the bottom, I had to wrap the robe tighter as it wanted to stay behind.

Pouring a cup of coffee, I felt excited. It was like Christmas with gifts looking at the trolley. I lifted the first lid to see what was hiding under it. I felt enthusiasm creeping in as I discovered not food but a brand-new phone under plate number one. Smiling, I sipped my coffee and took the box out of the plate.

Folding my legs on the bed, I opened the box and stared at the phone. It was brand new and a nice one as well. Holding the Oukitel phone in my hand felt like home. I placed it on the bed next to me and opened the second plate. This one actually had food in it. It was a plain breakfast with sausages, eggs, some muffins, mushrooms, and a piece of steak. The delightful aroma instantly filled the air around me.

My stomach growled. I hadn't realized how hungry I was until now. With everything that had gone on, I skipped supper altogether. Taking a bite from the muffin, I had to close my eyes. It melted in my mouth, infusing my senses with caramel chocolate and a hint of strawberry cream. It was to die for; I couldn't believe anything could taste that good.

I opened the last plate, not sure what to expect, but I was pleasantly surprised. It contained a single red rose with purple on the edges and a note. I picked up the rose and smelled it, and allowed its unique fragrance to fill my mind before opening the note. Reading it out loud, I pulled out the bag and placed it on the bed next to me. "You are the purest of roses. I hope you enjoy the gifts, and I am sorry. Yours always."

Picking up another muffin and biting into its velvety softness, I wondered what flavor this one was. It was extraordinarily creamy with a hint of caramel, mint, and chocolate.

Zipping the bag open, I was surprised to find it held a laptop inside. I thought Ashan was trying to spoil me as I took it out. Things may turn out to be better this time around. I should have run away sooner, I thought, grinning at myself.

My grin faded as my mind suddenly reminded me of the end results. Shaking off the gloom that was trying to take over, I breathed deeply. "No, you're not going to dwell on that," I reprimanded myself.

I opened the laptop and wondered if I should try to hack their system. Just for fun to see if it was now being monitored. Plus, it would help to take my mind off last night.

After finishing the second muffin, I decided to leave it alone. Placing everything down on the bed, I rose and headed to the bathroom. While washing and dressing, I couldn't make up my mind about what to wear. After a bit, I pulled on slacks and a top.

Sitting back down on the bed admiring my new toys, I heard a knock at the door. "Yes," I called out thinking that it could be Ashan. Although, I didn't know why he would knock.

The door opened and Cleo stuck her head in. "Morning," she said cheerily. Seeing her smiling face brightened the day even more.

"Hi, there," I replied as she opened the door fully.

"Ashan asked that you join him in his office." She added while collecting the trolley. "I hope you enjoyed your breakfast," Cleo added but left before I could reply.

Closing the laptop, I shoved the phone in my pocket and headed to the office, wondering why he would summon me instead of coming to see me. It could be that he was busy, I thought. The door was open when I came down the hall, so I just walked in, but I stopped just inside the doorway.

There were two other men there with him. I had seen them once or twice before and remembered the one from my rescue. I was sure he was Ashan's brother or at least family somehow. I wasn't sure of the other one. He could be a client. Yet, it felt more personal; maybe he was also family. I had read that the Morozov family is quite large.

"Jamie," Ashan said as he saw me. His smile this morning lit up his whole being. "This is my cousin Leo," he added, pointing at the one man I thought could be a client. "And this is my brother, Luder," he said, pointing to the other man.

I was right; the one is his brother. There was very little resemblance between the three though; I would never have made the connection. Both men smiled at me as they spoke almost in unison.

"Welcome to the family," they said and grinned at each other. I felt quite out of place. I expected Ashan to first talk to me and sort things out. Now, I was being introduced to his family. Who said I still wanted to stay?

I only wanted to return to the confines of the suite at that moment. I should have insisted that Ashan come to me. Standing there staring at the three men before me, my mind traveled away. Come to think of it, I haven't seen or heard Ana since I returned. I made a mental note to ask Cleo about it later.

The three men before me were all smiling at me, and I wondered what had happened in the seconds I was enthralled in my mind.

"Come in and sit with us," Ashan said, pulling his chair around his desk to join those already in front of it. Luder closed the door behind me, and we all sat down.

"So, then," Leo spoke first, "Ashan told us you're very skilled in your field, and I was wondering if you could tell us a little more about your expeditions?" Not sure what Ashan had told them I considered his

90

question. Ashan was pouring us each a drink and handed me one. Taking my glass, I took a big sip.

Leo was a tall man with dark hair and deep green eyes that softened his look. Glancing at Luder, I noticed he had two different colored eyes but was also tall. In build, I supposed Ashan and Luder were similar, but I felt sure that Ashan was taller, and they wore their hair differently.

"Okay, okay," Leo said anxiously. "What do you prefer? A backdoor, phishing, or brute force attack."

Stunned at his words, I felt my mouth open, but no words came out. Ashan had told them everything, I thought in disbelief. But as Leo continued to speak, I realized he also had to be a hacker. He knew way too much not to be.

Once we started talking in my language, I felt more at ease. It took a while and a lot of chatting, but I started to settle in. Leo and Luder were very friendly and seemed to accept me even though I had caused some issues.

Ashan and Luder mostly talked to each other as Leo, and I spoke about hacking. They added their two cents worth now and then but couldn't keep up. We had some more drinks, and lunch was brought to us. After lunch, Leo spoke about some of the new protocols on their network. He had put new ones in place should anyone try and hack them again.

Grinning, Leo looked me in the eye as he spoke. "You claim to be so brilliant. Let's see if you can hack us now."

I was astounded by the invitation. I had considered doing it earlier to see if I could, but I had not known then about the added security. But now, now, I was being asked to do it. "Okay," I replied, standing up and heading for the door. "Let me just go grab my laptop," I added, smiling at Ashan as I left the office.

I hadn't had much time to play with the laptop and wasn't sure it would have all I needed. But the time I had been on it was enough to know it could have everything on. Picking it up from the bed, I felt alive. I have always loved challenges. I rushed back to the office, where the three men waited for me.

Sitting opposite Leo at the table, I opened my new laptop. He had already set up his and waited for me to begin. As I started, the three men watched me closely; I could feel their eyes on me. I didn't let their stares faze me, though.

I infiltrated the network quickly but couldn't get to any real detail. I tried and tried pulling all the tricks I had from my hat. But no matter what I did, I couldn't get in. After about an hour, I sat back in my chair and threw my hands in the air. "Nice," I said, looking from one man to the other. "You did a stellar job, Leo."

Leo beamed at me as he spoke. "I reckon our data is safe, wouldn't you agree?"

I nodded, smiling at his childlike reaction. I reached out over the table to congratulate him, before catching Ashan's look. His posture had changed, and he suddenly seemed upset. I wasn't sure what was happening, but I saw his anger coming through as Leo, and I shook hands. For a second, the images of him beating Pedro played in my mind like a movie.

"Great stuff," Leo added. "Just let me know if you're interested in working for us exclusively, okay." As he finished, he winked at me.

I felt my cheeks turning crimson. Ashan stepped up to my side, breaking up our handshake. "She's mine, now stop this," he growled, looking harshly at Leo. I didn't like where this was heading and felt annoyed at him. I might be married to Ashan, but I didn't belong to him.

Slamming my laptop closed, I stood up rapidly. "Well, it was nice meeting you both," I said. "But I'm a bit tired now. I think I'll just head back to the suite."

Images of Pedro on the floor and Ashan on top of him tried to flood my mind. I fought hard to keep them from upsetting me further. I felt like screaming at him but would wait until we were alone.

Luder and Leo both nodded and said goodbye as I turned to the door. Ashan quickly moved to hold the door open for me. As I passed him, I gave him an angry glare hoping he would know what it was for.

I went back to the suite, angry at Ashan. Taking a long bath, I lay soaking in the herbal essence I added to my water. I lay soaking it up for a while. I cleared my mind and tried to relax. Once I was done, I went to bed.

Cleo came up with supper, but I didn't want any as I had heartburn. I was feeling a little ill as well. But I was sure it was just from everything that was going on. It could be from stress though, or something I had for breakfast or lunch. I wasn't sure, but I was confident that I would feel better in the morning.

Chapter 16 - Ashan

I waited for Jamie to leave before turning back to Leo. "What was that all about?" I spat at him. "She is mine, and as you know, I already married her."

"Slow down, Ashan," Leo stated as he rose. "I am very happily hitched, you know that. Man, I was just being friendly. As you said, she's officially part of the family. I'm sorry if you feel I was overly friendly. Constrain that beast, it's not a good look on you, and I'm sure she saw it as well."

"Brother," Luder said as he walked closer. "Calm down, as you have pointed out to me many times in the past; don't lose your head over a woman." Luder tapped me on the shoulder as he continued. "Follow your own advice here. Plus, do you really think Leo would make a pass at your wife, or anyone's wife for that matter?"

"Get a grip on this Ashan, or you'll lose her due to your actions, man," Leo added as he moved around the desk.

Feeling my mood slowly changing, I grinned at them. "Sorry, Leo," I said, walking back to my table. "It's just, after Ana and everything with Pedro, I don't know what's gotten into me." Lifting the bottle of whiskey, I continued. "Another drink?"

"Sure," they replied again in unison. We laughed and I was glad to have them there. Luder has always looked out for me; I may need him now more than ever. We shared a couple more drinks and discussed growing the business on my end before Leo eventually left.

Luder and I visited a while longer, and soon, noticed evening creeping up on us. As he was about to leave, he stopped at the door and turned back to me. "Ashan, if you really like Jamie. It's fine, and I'm glad for you. But please, don't become an obsessive bastard. Make sure you treat her right and consider her in everything you do."

I nodded, "Noted, thanks, Luder, you drive safe, and send Skyler my love. We'll get together soon so everyone else can also meet Jamie."

He waved before pulling the door closed behind him. After checking on operations throughout the den, I headed to the suite, eager to see if Jamie was okay. Once again, I had some explaining to do, I thought as I pushed the door open. Jamie seemed to already be sleeping when I got there.

Not wanting to disturb her, I decided we could talk in the morning. I quickly showered and moved cautiously as I joined her in the bed. I lay on one side briefly, then turned on the other. It was some time before I fell asleep as my mind replayed the last week and all that had happened in a loop.

Frustrated at myself, I considered getting up again. Turning over again, I lay watching her sleep. She was a vision, and sometime later, as I counted every movement of her chest, I drifted off.

I woke before her and ordered some breakfast and coffee for us. After taking a quick shower, I opened the door and waited for our food. Once it arrived, I quietly moved it into the room. I poured myself a cup of coffee and sat on the couch watching her.

Jamie looked like an angel lying there so calm and at peace. After what felt like an eternity but was more like five minutes, she moved. Turning to her back, she stretched out her arms and fluttered her eyes. I filled with a warmth inside as she turned and smiled softly at me.

She was safe here and she no longer appeared to be upset with me. As she pulled the sheets to one side and lowered her legs out of the bed, sitting up, I held out a cup of coffee for her. Jamie took the cup from me, closed her eyes as she brought it up to her lips and breathed in slowly.

Opening her eyes, she beamed at me. "Thank you," she said softly.

"No problem, hun," I replied, sitting back. "So, I was thinking," I started but she interrupted before I could continue.

"You," Jamie giggled as she spoke. "You were thinking. Well, that must be a first, I suppose."

Grinning at her, I reconned that I deserved that. I had been out of control the last week and a half. Lowering my head I spoke out. "I'm sorry Jamie, yes, I've been a bit hardheaded and difficult."

Looking up at her, I noticed her sparkle had returned as she responded while rubbing her chin and looking up. "Hardheaded and difficult aren't the words I would have used but okay."

"Tell me something about you?" I asked sipping some coffee before pulling the trolley in between us and opening the plates. "You hungry?"

Jamie's smile lit up the room as she moved closer and picked up the croissant. "It's not even Friday yet?" she said as she took a bite.

"No, but a little birdie told me you like these." I watched her close her eyes as she chewed, completely absorbed in the taste.

"Well, what would you like to know?" Jamie inquired after swallowing.

"Anything you are comfortable sharing with me, I want to know you."

She sat a while in silence enjoying her breakfast and I waited patiently. Once she had finished the croissant, she glanced at me and then flopped back on the bed.

"Before all this," she said, waving her hands in the air in a circle. "I had hoped to someday work for a computer company, to learn more and teach young minds." Jamie sat back up looking at me. "And you?"

This was a bit unexpected, and I was caught off guard. "Well," I said, trying to consider my reply. "I plan on building a gambling empire someday and hope to make my family proud."

Jamie smiled at me as she nodded. "What do you generally do for fun, in your off time, if I can call it that?" I asked, leaning forward.

"I used to play some online games, surf the net and so on. Nothing too exciting but since I got here, I noticed, I love swimming and chatting with the staff." She grinned as she spoke of her old and new life.

This was a side of her I had not seen. She spoke with passion as we talked more about activities and people. After a while, I left for my morning checks. Jamie was going to get dressed and meet me for lunch.

I considered showing her around town afterwards and maybe taking her out. The rest of the day went smooth, and she appeared to have a good time. Returning to the den, I was notified of issues in the top floor restaurant.

Jamie went ahead back to the suite as I attended to what was needed. By the time I got back to the room she was sleeping. Not wanting to wake her, I carefully crawled into bed and fell asleep.

Over the course of the next four weeks, we spent less and less time together. The den was a hive of activities and clients which was leaving me with little time spare. Jamie didn't seem to mind as her friendship with Cleo tightened.

It has been four weeks since the incident with Pedro and Jamie had settled nicely. Things at the den had also started calming and I had more time to spend with her again.

Luder and Leo had been on me to introduce her to the family, but I didn't think she was quite ready. I decided I would take her out and ask her about it over dinner. We arrived a bit early, but our table was ready.

On our way home, I popped the question. "Jamie, Leo and Luder asked if you wanted to meet the family?"

Glancing at me, she smiled. "Maybe, I'm not sure, what do you think?"

Shaking my head slightly, I replied. "It's up to you, whenever you feel ready."

"Okay, maybe over the weekend." She added before looking back out the window.

I accepted her answer and didn't push it. We were both tired when we arrived back, and Jamie headed upstairs while I checked in with the guards. Entering the suite, I found her sleeping. After a quick shower, I also lay down for the night.

Opening my eyes, I noticed the blinking red light of the clock and read the time. Three o'clock, it was still early in the morning. But something woke me; there was a sound in the room or close by. Glancing at Jamie's side, I saw she wasn't in bed anymore. No, where did she go, I thought as I sat up, rapidly glancing around the room. I saw the bathroom door halfway closed and heard the sound coming from there.

Getting up, I went to see what was going on, as I felt sure that Jamie was there. Pushing the door open, I saw her seated on the floor next to the toilet hanging over it. "Jamie," I spoke, feeling concerned as I walked closer. "Are you okay?"

She looked like someone who drank too much. Her face was only slightly lighter than usual, which I didn't understand as she only had one drink and then juice. She glanced up at me only for a second and mumbled into the toilet. She was throwing up; could it have been something she ate?

Stepping closer, I squeezed her shoulder. "Jamie, are you okay?"

Looking up at me, her eyes appeared a bit glazy. "Not sure," she mumbled and turned her head back down to the toilet.

"I'll get some water; I'll be right back," I said as I hastily went to the kitchen and poured her a glass of cold water. Walking back to the bathroom, I wondered. If not the drink or food, what could be causing this reaction?

We'd only been together once, but could it be? After I handed her the glass, I watched as she sipped at it. Counting the time, I realized it could actually be seeing that it has been just over five weeks. I quickly went downstairs and asked one of the guards to go buy a pregnancy test. For safety, let's rule out anything normal before I call the doctor.

A while later, I headed back up with the test in hand. Jamie was sitting on the corner of the bed, looking slightly paler than usual. I was sure it was from her session with Mr. Loo.

"Here," I said, handing her the test. "Just to be sure, we need to rule out any possibilities."

Jamie took the test and stared at it for the longest time. Glancing up at me she carefully shook her head. "No, can't be."

"Let's just make sure, if not, I'll call the doctor."

She sat a while longer staring at the test. As she eventually stood, I noticed she appeared slightly distracted, her entire upper body was slouched as she shuffled back to the bathroom. This was understandable; so much had happened in a short period.

"I'll just wait here," I called after her. I was hoping for an invitation but didn't want to intrude or push her. I had indeed done enough of that. She stopped at the door, glanced back at me, and nodded like someone sleepwalking.

Waiting for her to do the test and return felt like a lifetime passing. I was pacing the room, treading a line into the carpet. Then, the door finally opened, and Jamie came out, holding the test up in the air.

"Jamie," I asked as she walked toward me, but she looked like she was in more of a daze than when she went in. I couldn't read her, so I took the test from her as she plopped down on the bed. She still appeared a little off but now also seemed to have tears in her lovely eyes.

Staring at the lines on the test, I was shocked. We only had sex once, yet the results were positive. "We're pregnant?" I uttered in disbelief. My mind went blank for a second and then flooded with everything that had to be done.

"This is phenomenal," I said, pulling Jamie into my arms and turning a couple of times. Placing her back down, I beamed at her. "There's so much to do," I uttered, but she just stood there. "Jamie, aren't you happy?

Hearing the door open behind us I turned to see Frank standing there. "Boss," he said softly.

"Yes, yes, Frank, just a moment." Turning back to Jamie, I hugged her again and kissed her forehead. I was overjoyed but wasn't sure how she felt. Yet, the den was calling and I had to see what needed to be done. "Get back into bed, I'll have someone check on you in a bit, okay."

She didn't reply as she took the test from my hand and crawled onto the bed. I stood a moment longer, watching her as my mind tried to grasp the situation. We were going to have a baby. I really had to talk to Jamie but needed to sort some things first.

Heading to my office, Frank walked with me, giving me all the updates. He informed me of Pedro's progress and all developments around the den.

"Good, good, Frank," I started as we entered my office. "Can you send the chef up and ask Cleo to come and see me? There is a lot to do. Thank you"

Sitting at my desk, I called the family doctor first, as Jamie and the baby deserved only the best care. Once an appointment was made, I started making arrangements for meals, clothing, and everything else needed.

Consulting the chef, I gave clear orders so he could only provide her with fitting meals and to let me know if any issues arose. I asked Cleo to visit a maternity store and get some new clothing suitable for a woman with a baby growing in her.

Staring out the window, still overcome with joy, I knew things would have to change but deep down, I was afraid. The next couple of weeks were going to be demanding, but I have never backed down from a challenge before, and I won't do so now. Jamie and the baby needed me to be at my best.

CHAPTER 17 - JAMIE

I crawled back into bed, watching Ashan stroll out of the suite. At that moment, my life changed, all my plans flew out the door with him. I felt numb as reality settled in. I was now truly stuck here. No more running away and wanting to be free of all this, I was pregnant with his child.

If I left, the enemies would find me, and I couldn't put my baby in danger. For a moment, I just stared at the test in my hand. I pulled my legs up, turned to my side, and cradled them. What if Ashan became more obsessive? How would I handle all of this?

Laying in that position helped ease the nausea. I had no idea what to do and no knowledge of being pregnant or raising a child. The world had shrunk, and I was left in a little cocoon. I slowly dozed off again, even though my mind scrolled through endless images of life I would never see again. I was startled awake by a knock on the door.

Sitting up, I looked at my watch, it was almost midday, and I couldn't believe I'd slept so long. I still felt a little tired, but the nausea was gone now. Scooting down to the edge of the bed, I called out. "It's open, come in."

Cleo surprised me when she entered, all sunny and smiling. "Good morning, I hope you're feeling better?"

Rubbing the sleep from my eyes, I stretched out releasing the yawn that just popped out. "Yes, thanks, I am. What is all of this?"

She had brought up lunch. I had to admit that I was relieved it wasn't Ashan who had returned. Yes, we needed to talk, but with this on top of everything else, I just needed a moment to breathe even though things were settling well.

"We've heard the good news," Cleo stated as she lifted the cover off the plate and poured me a glass of juice.

"Oh, I didn't know Ashan had told everyone." My stomach turned as I thought of facing all my newly made friends. "Everyone?" I inquired, glancing up at Cleo.

"Well, I don't know," Cleo responded, pushing a golden lock of hair back behind her small ear. "I know he saw the chef and me, but I don't know who else."

A sigh escaped my lips as I brought the glass up and sipped at the juice.

"Aren't you excited?" Cleo asked, raising her brows.

"I'm not sure what to make of all this, to be honest," I replied, pulling the trolley closer. Staring at the meal before me, I wasn't even sure if I was hungry.

Cleo sat down next to me. She started asking questions about my favorite color, what kind of tops and bottoms I preferred wearing, what foods I liked, and more. Her line of questioning was a bit weird, and when I confronted her about it, she simply said she wanted to get to know me better. I accepted her answer but couldn't shake the feeling that something else was up.

As we spoke, I ate some of the food she had brought. My mind strolled to Ana and I just had to know. Turning to Cleo, I asked her. "Tell me, I haven't seen Ana around. You know why?"

Cleo stood abruptly, glancing around as if she was about to spill the beans. "You haven't heard?" she whispered.

Shaking my head, I scooted to the edge of the bed.

"Ashan sent her away, she's no longer working here and I heard from the guards that she wasn't allowed back here at all."

Stunned at this revelation I was speechless. Cleo quickly took the trolley and left with a 'see you later' as she pulled the door closed.

After having a propper meal for lunch, I felt a lot better and decided to go for a swim and a stroll on the upper decks. I decided that staying would be best for both me and our child. What life would I be able to offer a child anyway? Ashan had a lot more to offer. Besides with Ana out of the picture there wouldn't be any more issues, of this I was sure.

Vowing to myself to give him a chance to prove his worth, I spent the afternoon on the top deck, sauntering through baby sites online. I admired the furniture and clothing and made a list of items I wanted. It was a bit odd that Ashan wasn't hovering over me, but I welcomed the time alone. I could focus on myself and the precious life growing within me.

Leaving the suite earlier, I noticed two guards following me. They kept their distance but were there whenever I turned around. So, I was sure he at least knew where I was and what I was doing. Then, my suspicions were confirmed as my supper arrived on the deck. I thanked the waiter and quite enjoyed the supper even though there was an obvious increase in veggies on my plate.

Feeling tired, I decided to turn in early and headed back to the suite. The night went a bit better, and I only woke twice. Getting up the second time, I noticed it was past three and Ashan had not come to bed. I assumed the den was keeping him quite busy as there had been many nights he didn't come to bed. Not that I minded as it gave me more time and space to do things I loved. Plus, there was no fussing or overprotective to deal with.

The next day, I received a visit from a well-known specialist. It was a surprise when Cleo called me to Ashan's office for the doctor. Ashan sat with me and had quite a few questions regarding my health and the baby. As the doctor answered all the questions and went through everything with us, I realized that Ashan was genuinely concerned.

He sat next to me, holding my hand the whole time. It was a big change from the man I had seen up until now. I wasn't sure if it was due to the pregnancy or the present company, but I liked seeing him so caring.

"We'll need to do some blood tests and have an ultrasound done with our next appointment," the doctor said, handing Ashan two pieces of paper.

Ashan shook his head in agreement as he replied. "Sure thing, doc. We'll get these done in the week."

The doctor discussed meals, exercise, and daily care with us. He also made an appointment date for the next time but asked that we come to his office. Once he left, Ashan saw that everything was taken care of.

He ordered breakfast and asked that the chef come up to discuss my meals. The chef was a reasonably tall man, but exactly what one would expect. He had a big round face, a full head of sleek-back black hair, and a small beard. Even though he was reasonably tall, he had more than enough meat around his bones.

The chef was always smiling and friendly. I had never seen him down or upset. His white coat and hat fit him like a glove. Ashan asked him to sit with us as we had lunch.

"Right then," Ashan started. "What do you think would be best for meals during pregnancy?" he asked the chef.

The chef smiled wide at me as he spoke. "Congratulations." I smiled back at him and shook my head. "Well, we must have fruit, yogurt, vegetables, protein, and whole grains. What do you enjoy most?"

Thinking it over, I felt Ashan squeezing my hand. "I love mango, papaya, and cherries." The chef made notes in a small book he carried around in his shirt pocket as I spoke. "For my vegetables, I will have pumpkin, potato, and cauliflower."

"I would suggest we add broccoli, cabbage, and spinach to that list if you don't mind?" Chef asked.

Glancing down, I nodded but didn't love the idea. Vegetables weren't one of my favorite things, but I knew I had to get some in.

"Right then," the chef said as he rose. "For meats, we'll stick to mostly white meats such as fish and poultry."

Ashan stood and walked to the door with him. "Thank you," he added before closing the door behind the chef.

He called and arranged for a personal trainer for my exercise routines. It was all so surreal, and I had to pinch myself a couple of times to make sure I wasn't dreaming. This cold man actually had a heart which was warming, I thought as he moved back toward me.

Ashan sat back down but this time before me and not next to me. "Hun," he said, taking my hands in his. "I am very excited, but I want you to be comfortable and taken care of. If there is anything you want, just let me know, okay?"

His eyes softened as he spoke and I could see he cared deeply. "Additionally, you will have two more guards at your disposal. If there is anything, you just ask them." Ashan assured me they would always be around if I needed help.

"I have arranged with Cleo to be by your side when I am busy." He added, leaning forward and giving me a tender kiss on the cheek.

We met with the personal trainer just before supper time and he would be back in the morning to get started. We would have three sessions a week, one for dancing, one for yoga, and another for pilates. Every other day I would stick to swimming.

I felt tired just thinking about it but knew it was important for both me and the baby. Once again Ashan didn't come to bed, but when I opened my eyes the next morning, Cleo was there waiting with my vitamins and breakfast.

Cleo became my left hand over the next three weeks. She was there when I opened my eyes and, most of the time, also the last person I saw before bedtime. Ashan was gentle, caring, and understanding moving forward and I felt sure that with each passing day, he became softer and more caring.

Most of my nausea had dissipated and I was feeling quite well as I got dressed for our doctor's appointment. It has now been eight weeks and the doctor insisted we come in once a month for now.

As I ascended the stairs, I saw Ashan waiting for me in the lobby. "Good morning hun," he said, taking my hand and kissing my cheek. "How did you sleep?"

Smiling up at him I nodded, "Good, thanks and you?"

"Always good, but you know that." He mumbled as we headed out to the car. The trip to the doctor's office went quickly. Today would be our first sonar to see and hear the baby. Entering the enormous dark grey building that held the offices, I beamed at Ashan as he took my hand. It was an exciting day.

From the reception desk you could see three doors to the back but from the bright sign stuck to the desk, I noted that there had to be more as there were five names on it. The the right of the desk was a sign haning from the roof that read 'Doctor's Offices'. To our left the sign hanging read 'Xray, Sonar, Ultrasound, and Pharmacy'.

The elderly lady behind the large half-moon desk smiled as we came to stand before her. "Your first time, dear?" she inquired, handing Ashan a clipboard with papers and a pen.

Filled with excitement and fear at the same time, I battled finding words so I just shook my head and smiled at her. "Good for you, such young love is incredible." She added.

Ashan handed her the board back, having completed the documents and we took a seat waiting to see the doctor.

"You've been quite busy the last three weeks," I commented while we waited.

Ashan squeezed my hand again as he lifted and kissed my fingers. "I was, yes," he said. Taking a deep breath he continued. "I wasn't sure if you wanted space but felt you might need it?"

I was completely surprised by the sudden change but enjoyed it. I had little to no worries in the world and spent my days doing whatever I wanted. Cleo and I became good friends as I learned more about her life and her dreams. We both found it a bit odd that I had not met any of Ashan's other family. It almost felt like he didn't want them close to me.

It wasn't an issue, though, as I would most likely not even know what to do with so many people fussing over me and the baby. I liked having space and not caring about other people's impressions of me or their needs.

But after a while, the space became lonely. Spending my days with basically only Cleo around and two guards following me wasn't enough anymore.

"Yes, I did, and do," I mumbled, looking down at our entwined fingers. "But, I would also like to spend some more time with you."

Hearing our names being called we looked up. A nurse in blue and white uniform stood under the sign that lead to the doctor's offices and was calling for us. Rising and moving forward I felt Ashan pulling me back. "I'll do better," he said before walking toward the nurse.

Entering the office my nose tickled from the smell of eucalyptus oil. The doctor wore a white coat and was seated behind his desk. He stood and walked over to us as holding out his hand to Ashan.

"Please, don't sit, come with me." He said, walking out the door. We followed him down the hall and through a short passage to another room. Opening the door, he stepped aside as he spoke. "Please come in and Jamie, you can take a seat on the bed for us."

The odor in this room was quite a contrast from his office. It reeked of cleaning material and disinfectants. The narrow white leather covered bed was speckless and almost sparkled as if it was new.

Next to it stood a box-like machine with wires and what looked like a remote of somekind. The surface of the bed was a bit hard but comfortable none the less.

"Please lay back and lift your shirt slightly for me," the doctor said as he turned the machine on. "This might be a bit cold," he added before squirting a clear liquid onto my tummy.

We watched in amazement as he moved with the remote object across the liquid. He stopped a couple of times taking measurements and images. Once this was done, he turned on the sound and we could hear our baby's heart beat.

Ashan squeezed my hand as I gasped and fought the tears that suddenly appeared out of nowhere. Filling with excited energy I wanted to dance around the room. It was the most precious moment of my life.

"Well, all looks good and the baby is growing nicely." The doctor said grinning at us as he wiped off my stomach "You can make another appointment for next month and let me know if you have any questions." He added as he left.

After making the appointment, Ashan took me shopping and made sure I got all I wanted.

It was lovely, over the next two weeks we had days that were loaded with fun, but the loneliness crept back in, and soon I realized I wanted more. I also wanted Ashan's company, not just flings of shopping and dinners, I wanted him to spend time with me. Once the new phase wore off, I started feeling sad.

Strange enough, but I started missing him more each day. Ashan had been treating me as an equal, and I had to admit that I was even missing our arguments. I couldn't explain it even if I tried, I saw him at least once every morning and night just before bedtime, as he would check in on me. But I felt alone, empty somehow as if something had left my life.

Tonight, I decided to wait for him. Another two weeks had passed. I was now twelve weeks pregnant and I needed some loving not just highlights. When Ashan came in shortly after eight, I was seated on one of the chaise lounges.

"You still up?" he asked as he came closer and knelt before me, taking my hands into his.

"I waited for you," I replied turning my gaze down as my mouth pulled into a smile. "Will you stay the night and just hold me?"

Rising, Ashan pulled me up into his warm embrace. "Sure thing." Slipping my arms around him we just stood for a while. I felt safe and at home in his arms as a sense of peace flooded me. Ashan picked me up and walked to the bed without a word.

After laying me down, he got in behind me and pulled me close into his reassuring embrace. I breathed in deeply as his sweet, honeyed aroma filled the air around us. Closing my eyes, sleep came quickly.

Waking, I was filled with blissfulness I didn't know existed. I was walking on clouds for a day or two, but as the days passed, it faded. Ashan had returned to his normal routine of visiting, outings, and meals. He didn't stay in the evenings.

Confused and frustrated, I wasn't sure what to make of his actions as days turned into weeks again. We had another visit with the doctor at sixteen weeks. The baby was doing great and so was I. Yet, my stomach had started growing and the facts could no longer be hidden.

Ashan took me for another wardrobe fitting and filled my closet with suitable clothing for the next trimester. After dinner, I had a long soaking bath. As I lay relaxing, I felt it for the first time. Thrilled, I couldn't wait for Ashan to come up.

I was excited to see him as the baby had started moving, and I just had to share the news. Ashan arrived on schedule, and when he entered, I jumped into his arms. He held me for a moment, and I felt whole.

"You have to feel this," I whispered in his ear.

He gently took me by the hips and pushed me back. "Feel what? What's going on? Are you okay? Should I call the doctor?" He asked, and I heard some concern in his voice.

"It's nothing to worry about, silly," I replied, beaming. "Feel here," I added as I pulled his hand closer and held it against my stomach.

My attention was on his face as I felt the baby softly licking. His lit up as he felt the light movement. "Ashan," I said staring at his handsome face. His eyes were filled with compassion as he looked back at me. His hands were warm as he wrapped them around me. "Will you stay the night and just hold me?" I asked.

He nodded in agreement as he leaned in and kissed me tenderly. Pulling away, I looked down at the floor to my foot as I twisted my toes left and right, suddenly feeling shy. Turning, I moved to the bed and crawled up to my place.

Ashan lay down beside me. He moved up against my back first, just holding my stomach. Feeling him holding me, his soft touch, and the heat he was giving off, started to turn me on.

As we lay, I became more and more restless, my body tingled, and I knew I wanted his touch. No, I had to have it. Ashan stroked my hair, waiting for me to fall asleep, I suspected, but I just couldn't. Having him so close, his touch, it was almost too much, it was messing with my hormones.

His touch, his smell, and his body heat were all warming me on the inside. Eventually, I took his hand from my belly and pulled it up, placing it over my breast and cupping his hand with mine. Ashan lay dead still for a moment.

He slowly pulled his hand out from under my arm and turned on his back. I glanced over my shoulder at him. His eyes were closed but I knew he wasn't sleeping yet as he had a smile on his face. How could he, I was sure he also wanted more than just to cuddle.

Turning to him, I laid my head on his chest. Ashan embraced me in his arms, holding me tight, but I still couldn't fall asleep. I wanted his touch, I needed him.

I felt like I was going to explode as I rubbed my legs together. How did he notice, I wondered as I placed a hand on his firm abs. This made me even hotter, a tingling sensation shot through me, igniting fires all over my body. I moved my fingers left and right over his abs swallowing hard as I tried to contain my urges.

CHAPTER 18 - ASHAN

Getting into bed with Jamie, I felt amazing. The baby was moving, but she wanted me there, which made me happy. I was trying my best to lay still, to just offer her comfort and sleep, as I didn't think she would want anything more.

I had heard stories and read that many women actually get more needy during pregnancy, and then others simply aren't interested in sex anymore. Not truly knowing her all that well yet, I was unsure of what to expect. Laying there beside her, Jamie was making it very hard for me to sleep. She was restless, and every move she made turned me on.

Her hair smelled of sweet spring blossoms. The pregnancy has given her a sensational glow that I couldn't explain. I was glad that she and the baby were healthy and happy. I would give her the world if that was what she wanted.

The passing weeks had been difficult. Giving her space and staying away was not my idea of fun, but I knew it was needed. Jamie had to find her way, and I didn't want to put her under any more pressure than she had.

Now, lying beside her, feeling her body next to mine, I wanted her more than ever. But considering her needs were more important than mine. Yet, as she played with her fingers on my chest, she stirred everything inside me. Placing a hand under her chin, I pulled her head up slowly.

"Jamie, what's wrong? Can't you sleep?" I asked, smiling at her. She seemed a bit irritated at me. I noticed she was biting down on her lower lip. I felt her leg moving up and down against mine. If she only knew what she was doing to me, how much I wanted to make love to her in that moment.

"Nothing," Jamie responded, turning out of my arms and away from me. I wasn't sure what I had done in the short time from entering up until now that could have upset her, but I felt guilty anyway.

Turning on my side facing her back, I touched her shoulder and spoke softly. "Jamie, I'm sorry if I said or done something wrong."

"No, it's not you," she replied, almost whispering. Something was different; her voice sounded different as she spoke. She felt stiff and didn't move.

I stroked her arm, moving closer in the process. "Jamie, what can I do to help? Is there anything you need or want?" I asked, kissing her shoulder softly and taking her hand in mine. She moved subtly with every kiss.

"Ashan," she whispered. "I'm sorry, it's just, well, it's my hormones. I don't know what's going on with me or why."

"Oh, baby, it's okay," I replied, turning her to her back in my arms. "Mood changes are common, I think, or so I've read."

Jamie turned her head away, and I noticed her cheeks turning pink as she spoke. "It's not just the moods. I, well, I need more from you than just sleeping in the same bed." She closed her eyes for a second and licked her lips.

How could I have been so stupid? I felt her leg moving up and down, and she was trying to tell me what she wanted when she placed my hand on her breast. But she didn't want a mere cuddle; she wanted sex. I thought she was upset with me. I knew hormones could cause fluctuations in mood, but creating a need for sex was something I didn't know. Was it safe? Could I hurt her or the baby? I would make sure to call the doctor and ask him tomorrow.

"I don't know, what's going on. I can't help these feelings. I've tried through." she said, thrusting her head into my chest. "I have all these feelings and don't know what to do."

"It's okay, baby, I'll make you feel better," I added, kissing her face. Turning her onto her back, I noticed she was blazing; her beauty was breathtaking. Jamie breathed out deeply as I moved my hands over her voluptuous breasts.

I wanted to satisfy all her carnal needs. Being a hotblooded man, her luscious curves turned me on fire. But tonight was all about her needs and desires. Taking a long and slow breath, I calmed the spirit within and focused on her.

Pulling the covers from the bed, I moved Jamie to the middle. "You just lay back and relax, baby," I said as I stood over her on my hands and knees.

First, I bent forward and kissed her forehead, then moved down to each cheek before kissing her on the mouth. Jamie pushed her hands into my hair, holding my head firmly as the kiss intensified. Having to come up for air after a bit, I pulled her hands down one by one.

"Let me continue," I whispered as I kissed her chin. She smiled, and I felt her legs moving left and right below me. Pushing up on one hand, I used the other to slowly push the thin strap of her nightgown over her shoulder. First, the one and then the other. Coming upright on my knees, I pulled them further down and over her hands.

Her firm breasts were revealed, and her dark pink nipples stiff as the fabric moved down. I shifted backward, pulling her nighty with me. I ended up standing at the foot of the bed, dropping it to the ground. Leaning forward, I kissed her belly and made two lines up the outside of her thighs to her panties.

Taking hold of her underwear on both sides, I took my time to pull them down. Every inch they moved, exposing her more, was blessed with a warm, tender kiss. Jamie released a deep sigh as I kissed the top of her pussy, pulling the panty free and down her legs just to drop them on the floor as well.

Looking at her, my body ached out of lust. She lit up the entire room with her smile. Laying down next to her on my side, I drew a line up her leg. Jamie closed her eyes, breathing out loudly as she wiggled her other leg.

Pushing up on one arm, I drew a line up her other perfect thigh before leaning toward her and kissing her neck. She squirmed around as my hand moved up over her pussy and onto her breast. There was nothing I wanted more than to pin her to the bed and repeat our first time. But I couldn't, I promised to ease her hunger, and that was what I was going to do.

As I kissed down her neck, my fingers moved in wavy lines over her stomach towards her pussy. Jamie moaned and arched her back as I slid my hand between her legs. Using one finger, I slowly parted the lips, rubbing up and down. She parted her legs a little more every time I moved up and down.

Leaning over her, I sucked her nipple into my mouth. Jamie grabbed my head as another moan escaped her. Nibbling her nipple, I slid a finger into her. Her legs parted more, allowing me greater access.

Sliding my finger between her folds, feeling how wet she was for me sent a rush through my body. I licked her breast and sucked her nipple again, but this time, I bit down softly. Jamie moaned harder, and her breathing was slightly rushed. Hearing her moan and feeling her hands pulling at my hair brought my dick to almost full attention.

Taking a deep, steady breath, I tried to control my urges as I laid kisses down her stomach. Pushing her legs wider apart, I moved off the bed, caressing her legs. Jamie smiled down at me as I moved my hands up and down her inner thighs.

She grabbed the bed sheets on both sides of her head once I moved in between her legs and softly sucked at her pussy. Releasing, but not moving away, I licked her. Jamie squirmed closing her legs around my head.

Grabbing the insides of her thighs, I pushed her legs sideways and pinned them on the bed. Smiling up at her, I spoke tenderly. "No, no, no. Relax."

Jamie giggled as my fingers walked halfway up her inner thighs. Ensuring that she couldn't close her legs on me again, I moved back between her legs. I softly nibbled the top of her pussy, feeling her clitoris coming to life before licking her again.

She twisted around as deep moans pushed through her closed lips. Glancing up Jamie had pulled her lower lip into her mouth and moved her head from side to side with every move I made. Pushing myself up, I kissed her breasts again and sucked her nipples. After ravishing them, I trailed tender bites down her sides back to her pussy.

Lightly holding Jamie down, I started licking her intensely, moving faster and faster between her lips. Soon, I started tasting her juices with my tongue, and the wetter she got.

Her finger curled into my hair, as I started licking more forcefully. After a while, Jamie's breathing became jiggered, and she started begging for more. And I just gave her what she was asking for. At first, I inserted a finger into her while I made turns to lick and nibble her clitoris.

She lifted the top half of her body and slammed back to the bed, with each movement moaning louder and louder. Pulling my finger out, I fucked her with my tongue, pushing in as far as I could. Soon she was practically screaming for me to fuck her. I alternated between fucking her with my fingers and my tongue. While I had my fingers inside of her, I licked and sucked on her clitoris.

I could tell when she was close, as her hands tightened in my hair. She screamed as she came, and I licked up her juices through it all. My pounding dick released in my pants as I started slowing down enjoying her every breath and movement.

Jamie let go of her hold of her hold on my head and spread her arms out to her sides. Breathing in deeply. I knew that a shot shower was the only thing we still needed before sleeping. Walking to the side of the bed, I lifted Jamie into my arms. She flung hers around my neck and laid her head against my chest as I walked to the bathroom.

Once we were bathed and snug in our robes, we cuddled in bed. Holding her tight, I felt her relaxing and fall asleep.

Chapter 19 - Jamie

After my morning water workout, I joined Ashan for breakfast.

"The family's gathering this afternoon, and I thought it would be the perfect time for you to meet everyone," Ashan said as his second coffee arrived.

Almost choking on a strawberry, I tried smiling as I nodded. "The entire family?" I questioned after taking a sip of water.

"Yes, it'll be fun, you'll see," Ashan added as he rose and kissed my forehead. "Be ready by one."

I watched as he walked off to take care of the den's daily business. Swallowing hard at the lump in my throat, I felt my nerves spiking.

After breakfast, I went to the suite trying to decide what to wear. I was clearly showing, and everything made me look fat. After rummaging through everything, I finally decided to wear an ocean-green romper. It had soft grey wavy lines running from the top to the bottom. Looking in the mirror, I appreciated the lines, they made me look smaller, almost normal.

Under the romper, I wore a white tube top and my white sneakers. Feeling comfortable enough, I went down and ordered a double-thick milkshake. Generally, I only drank plain vanilla, but in the last couple of days, I found that my taste preferences had changed. Today I was having bubblegum, and tomorrow I might try the strawberry one or lime; it depended on how I felt.

I enjoyed my milkshake while I waited for Ashan to finish up. Ashan came out dressed in black jeans, a white button shirt, and white sneakers.

He looked so handsome. But some of the buttons were loose. I didn't like him showing off his chest, it reminded me of when we met and that brought back memories of Ana. So I buttoned them up as he came to stand by me.

Ashan just smiled at me as we got in the car and drove out of the parking area. I expected him to complain or stop me, but he didn't. We arrived at Leo's house shortly after one.

The place was stunning. I had never been to a house so extravagant. Before the door was a fountain with a statue of a man riding a horse. The fountain was surrounded by a rainbow of color made up of small flowers. The house itself appeared to have three or four floors. There were so many windows that I couldn't even begin to know how many rooms it held.

The house sat in the middle of the property, with lawns spreading left and right. To the outer edges, I saw lines of trees with more rainbow flowers breaking the overpowering green. The parking area ran along the lawn to both sides of the house. There were cars lined up outside the mansion entrance, almost filling all the parking spaces.

Seeing all the cars, I recalled that there would be many people as they were the most powerful Bratva in Miami. Feeling a bit out of place, I clung to Ashan as we moved around, and he introduced me. Glancing around, I could see some resemblances here and there, especially between the men.

These, I felt sure, were brothers and cousins. Then there were about three groups I could discern that were surely related to each other but were a more indirect family, like cousins once removed or something.

Everyone was overly friendly and welcomed me openly to the family. No one asked me about hacking or any related skills. There was no probing and prodding into what I did for a living. They all wanted to know about me, what I enjoyed doing in my free time, and the pregnancy.

Once all the introductions were made, Sam invited me to sit with some of the women. I met Evelina and learned she was Leo's twin. She was also a very capable wizard with computers and a risk taker. We seemed to have a lot in common.

We sat with Karine, Irina, and Skyler. Most of them already had kids and were excited for Ashan and me. As they shared some of their experiences, my ears stopped working as my focus was elsewhere. I couldn't stop watching Ashan and barely heard any of the conversation.

He seemed more at ease than I've ever seen him. He was playing around with some of the kids in between and was surprisingly good with them. My heart swelled with love, watching him in this calming element of his.

I saw another side of Ashan, and it was enlightening. I knew at that moment that he would make an excellent father. After lunch, everyone went their own way back to their lives and responsibilities.

As we drove back, I couldn't help but smile. I leaned over and squeezed Ashan's leg. Ashan glanced at me, grinning. "Your family is great," I said.

"Thanks," Ashan replied. "Any chance I will be meeting yours in the near future?"

"Well," I responded, swallowing hard as I turned away and stared out the window, I was hesitant, how would I explain it all? I was filled with apprehension just thinking about it.

"It's okay if you're not ready to share," Ashan stated, gently patting my hand.

Smiling at him, I decided to simplify it. "It's complicated," I continued, Swallowing the lump in my throat. "I've never really had a family or anyone I could depend on. I've always only had to rely on myself. My mother and father weren't really in the picture, and my aunt who raised me, well, she died when I was twelve."

Ashan sighed as we pulled into the den parking lot. "I'm so sorry, Jamie." He said, turning to me.

"It's not your fault, but that's why I hid my identity for most of my life. I had to protect myself and learn how to take care of myself. I didn't want pity or handouts."

"Still," Ashan said as he got out and walked around, opening my door. "I'm sorry that life has been so hard for you. Someone as amazing as you don't deserve such heartache." Blushing, I glanced away so he couldn't see.

He ordered some biscuits and cocoa, as well as fruit and cream, as we headed to the suite. Entering the suite, I took a quick shower and dressed more comfortably. Ashan got our order for the door for us before also taking a shower.

As we sat drinking hot cocoa and having biscuits with fruit on the bed, we continued to get to know each other.

"Now that you've met everyone, you know you have a family," Ashan mumbled while swallowing a bite.

I did, and it felt good. Smiling at him, I spoke, "So, the den, what's your plans?"

Finishing his biscuit and placing his cup down, he moved closer to me. He took my hands and kissed them before talking. "Everyone has their businesses and what they bring to the family."

I nodded as he spoke passionately. "Well, the gambling den is the one thing that's mine. I want it to flourish so everyone can be proud." His voice was filled with sincerity as he continued. "And the workers, they have become my friends, I want them to be happy and to make sure they can keep their jobs."

Ashan spoke about the den, his family, and the workers with so much emotion and compassion. He opened up and showed me a side of him that I truly liked. He wasn't your typical tough, bad guy. No, there was a lot of heart underneath the cold, icy exterior.

He was so soft and gentle. I knew that I had to tell him everything. If this was going to work, Ashan needed to know the whole lot.

"Ashan," I said, holding his hands tightly. "There's something I have to tell you." I swallowed hard and hoped he wouldn't get too mad at me for not telling him about my relations with Pedro earlier. "Some time ago, I got into a really sticky situation and needed a way out."

He smiled supportively at me. "Okay," he said and waited for me to continue.

Glancing down, I continued. "I got very drunk one night and had some trouble. To get out of the situation, Pedro offered me his help, but I had to sleep with him in exchange."

Looking up into his eyes, I continued hastily. "I regret my actions and what I had done, and I'm sorry for not telling you sooner." Once the words were out, I felt a little better; there were no secrets to worry about.

Ashan lifted my hands and kissed them again. "It's okay, baby," he said, pulling me closer. He hugged me tightly as he continued. "You only did what you had to, to survive. But that's over, and you now have me. You can rely on me, and you never have to hide again, I promise."

I felt relieved and safe in his arms. Tears of joy rolled down my cheeks as he tilted my head up and kissed me. His lips were warm, and his touch so gentle. I felt my stomach looping, as I wanted him.

Tenderly, he lowered me onto the bed as he continued to kiss me. A hunger inside me grew as he gave life to my desire for him. Ashan used one hand to unbutton the romper on my shoulders. He carefully pushed his hands slightly in behind my back and pulled the romper down. It went smoothly over my sneakers due to the wide pipes.

Ashan laid warm kisses on my belly as he pulled the thong down over my legs. Sitting up, fueled by my throbbing pulse and lust. I made quick work of ripping his shirt to undress him. Buttons went flying through the air.

As my lust increased, my patience shrunk. He assisted me in unbuttoning his belt and removing his jeans quickly, as well as his underwear. I grabbed him by his neck, pulling him down onto the bed with me while kissing him deeply.

Ashan then kissed his way down my body moving past my pussy to my thighs. It felt like he was teasing me as he kissed my inner thighs. This drove me through the roof as I felt like screaming. I struggled to control the insatiable need for him rising within me.

Moving back over my body, Ashan kissed my stomach, making it turn wildly, my breasts, my neck, and then finally my mouth. With each kiss, I felt my insides tumbling and my body burning with pleasure and desire.

Tenderly, he lowered himself into me while his tongue explored my mouth to its fullest. Filled with strong yearning, I felt my hands curling into his back and my nails digging into his skin as he slowly pulsed inside me.

My desire and lust grew with each gentle move, driving me up the wall. After a couple of intense pulses, I placed my hands on his chest and pushed him back. "Ashan, flip over, please." I breathed out, overcome with incredible yearning. He turned to his back, and I mounted him like the stallion he was.

Sitting upright on my knees, I pushed my hands into my hair. Ashan grabbed my hips as I rose up and down on his penis, hastily moaning out of pure bliss. After a couple of hard pulses, his hands moved up over my stomach to stroke my breasts. Cupping them, he played with one finger over the nipples, sending shudders through me.

As all my senses lit up, I couldn't control the moans that fled from my mouth. Reaching down, I pulled Ashan up into my arms. He sucks at my nipples as his strong hands cup my butt. My fingers flow through his thick hair while I push my feet onto the bed, raising to my hunches. Ashan let out a soft moan as I pushed up and lowered myself quickly back onto his lap.

He assisted by lifting me as I rode him feeling my pussy pulsing with each move. After a while, Ashan grabbed me tightly, moving to the end of the bed before he stood, lifting me with his strong arms. He turned around back to the bed. Ashan softly placed me back down before flipping me over onto my stomach and kneeling behind me on the bed.

Spreading my legs, he entered me from behind. I pulled the sheets into my mouth, trying to stifle my cries of satisfaction as Ashan moved in quick pulses. Slowing down, he pulled me up with him into the doggy position.

This time, his movements were slower. He slapped my ass lightly, sending shivers through my senses. Just as I thought he was done, he pushed my head back down to the bed and traced gentle lines over my back with his fingers before slapping my rear again.

"Baby," I whispered over my shoulder. "Ride me hard, fuck me, baby."

Ashan leaned forward and grabbed hold of my hair. As he carefully pulled my head up, he rammed into me. Exhaling hard, I pleaded for more. "Don't stop, baby, come on, give it to me."

He slapped my ass harder this time before taking hold of my hips and pumping me. His breathing was jiggered as he moved quicker and quicker. After a couple of wild drives into me, I felt him straighten up as he held me tightly against him for a second.

I felt my pussy pumping hot sticky liquid out over his balls. My mind felt like it was melting, my body trembled, and I climaxed.

Moving slowly twice more, I felt Ashan cum in me. He moaned between slow breaths. I felt his grip on my hips loosen, and he moved backward off the bed. Sliding forward, I allowed myself to lay back down as my breathing recovered. Turning, Ashan was standing by the foot-end of the bed, staring at me.

"You're amazing," he said softly as he held out his hand to me.

Giving him my hand, he pulled me up into his arms. Our bodies were sweaty, and we kind of stuck to each other as we kissed. Ashan picked me up and carried me to the shower. Once we had bathed and dressed, I pulled the sheets from the bed while he collected a fresh set.

Ashan held me in his warm embrace as we fell asleep.

Chapter 20 - Ashan

Some time during the night I must have turned as I was staring at the wall. Rolling over I placed a tender kiss on Jamie's cheek. Her eyes fluttered open as she turned her head and looked at me. "Morning hun, did you sleep well?" I asked stroking her cheek.

Beaming she nodded. "I was thinking, a quick shower before I headed to my office and once I was done with the morning checks and emails, we could grab breakfast?"

Jamie slid out of bed and headed for the bathroom without a word. I followed grinning. Watching her walk before me I felt a warm glow filling me. She was the most beautiful woman and being pregnant suited her. Yet, I felt saying that to her would most likely be offensive so I kept it to myself.

Once we finished showering, I headed down for my morning check. Jamie said she would meet me downstairs for breakfast. Once I was done with the check-in, I went to my office and called the doctor. He confirmed that sex was actually a good thing during pregnancy. Feeling more at ease, I continued with my emails.

Jamie entered my office about an hour later as I was finishing my emails and ready to join her downstairs. She was dressed in one of the dancer's outfits. "Oh my," I huffed at her as she placed a cup of coffee down before me. "May I ask what you been up to, or where you are going?" I said, slapping her behind.

Jamie walked back to the door in the glittering black gown. It fit her like it was part of her skin. Her breasts notably displayed some cleavage as they struggled to stay within the confines of the skimpy top.

Her legs exploded out of the dress with each step as they peeked through the slits on the sides. She walked out and glanced back as she was pulling the door closed. "If you can find me, well, let's see, what's on the menu" She whispered, licking her luscious lips before disappearing.

I was instantly aroused. My veins filled with burning lava. She was turning sex into a game, and my desire for her overtook me. Taking a sip of coffee, I rose from my table, wobbly on my legs as desire flooded me. I liked the idea of looking for her, of hunting her.

Dressed like that, I felt sure she would be upstairs in one of the private rooms. Wiping the sweat unexpectedly forming on my brow, I hoped no one else saw her out in the halls dressed like that. Yet, it was still early and most of the workers hadn't even arrived.

As I moved from one room to another without luck, I had to rethink her clothing. I had to try and figure out where Jamie could be hiding. I returned to my office and considered all the rooms and areas the den offered. I checked my office and noticed the passage door was slightly ajar. I was sure it was closed earlier.

Yes, of course, why didn't I look there first, I thought, entering the passage and locking the door behind me. She wouldn't be walking around outside dressed like that. Walking down the passage, I heard soft music playing. Following the music, I found a note pasted to a glass of whiskey in the conference room.

Picking the glass up, I pulled the note free and took a big sip, feeling my mouth suddenly dry. *'Turning, turning, washing and drying, where am I,'* the note read. Pushing my hand through my hair, I considered her words. Yes, I spoke to the walls as I turned and headed out. It was Wednesday, and the laundry staff didn't come in today, so the place would be empty.

Hurriedly, I walked down to the laundry room. Pushing the door open, I grinned as I found her. Jamie was seated on one of the large industrial washers. She beamed as I entered, closing the door behind me. "It took you a while," she said in a silky-smooth tone.

She sat with her legs open, the middle piece of the dress hanging down between them, exposing her soft legs on both sides. Walking briskly to her, I felt my dick coming to life.

123

Swallowing hard, I replied. "Yes, I was misled for a moment."

Jamie giggled as she grabbed my tie when I was within reach and pulled me close. Her kiss was heated and penetrating as she loosened my tie and unbuttoned my shirt. Her hands traveled down my chest, sparking all my senses as if they were filled with lighting. As she worked at my belt and pants, I pushed my hands up the sides of the dress, intending to rid her of any underwear.

Reaching her hips, I felt no fabric there; she wasn't wearing any undergarments. My heart did a flip as blood rushed through it and streamed south to my dick. My pants dropped to the floor, pulling my underwear with it as Jamie pushed it over my throbbing dick and down my hips.

She leaned back on the washed and placed her feet on the edges as she whispered. "What you waiting for, an invitation?"

Taking hold of the cloth draped between her legs, I lifted it, revealing her light pink rose. Placing the centerpiece of the dress to her side I bent down and licked her pussy. She was drenched, her sweet-salty moisture kissed my lips like the early morning breeze coming in over the ocean and lapping at the beach.

"Oh, baby," Jamie moaned, letting her head fall backward between her shoulder blades. "I crave for more of you."

If she only knew how strong my hunger for her was at that moment. I drew a line over the rim of her pussy with my tongue, enjoying watching her arch. Her moans were like music driving my passion.

Sticking my tongue into her pussy I sucked at her clitoris, tasting her magnificent juices. Jamie lifted her pussy as I sucked and opened her legs more, allowing my tongue deeper access. Her pure tenderness blanked out my mind, and I felt the beast within taking over.

I thrust my tongue deeper into her as she lifted more. Pulling out, I softly sucked her clitoris into my mouth and held it between my teeth as my tongue played with it. Jamie let out a raging scream as her arms flopped out to the sides, and her back met the cold steel of the machine.

Her feet came up to my shoulders, and I had to grab hold of the machine as she pushed it onto my shoulders. I felt her pussy pumping hot sticky liquid out onto my chin as her shrieks of satisfaction strengthened and she came.

Gasping for air, Jamie lifted her head and smiled. Stepping in closer, I shoved my rock-hard dick into her succulent ocean. Feeling the cave closing around my penis sent my senses into a whirlpool. Arching back as I started moving in slow, consecutive thrusts, I lifted her legs over my shoulders.

With each move, I felt the fires igniting within. Jamie lay moaning while my fingers played with her clitoris as I fucked her. After a couple of slow, soft thrusts, I felt my body starting to spasm. Grabbing hold of the washer, I must have pressed something as it came on beneath her.

It added a splendid vibration to our heightened sensations. Jamie was literally vibrating where she lay. With every push into her, I felt the washer's cold surface vibrate against my balls. The sensation was electrifying as I moved faster and fucked her harder. But it didn't take long for it to drive me over the edge.

Roaring, I pulled her hard onto my shaft, spitting like a cobra into her ocean. Jamie shook as she came with me. I just stood waiting for the waves to calm down momentarily before pulling out and stepping back.

Gasping in the air, I lifted her off the washer and stopped its operation. Pulling her into my embrace, I waited for her breathing to normalize before picking her up. Carrying her back up to our suite, I felt alive and invigorated. I loved the challenges she brought, and today was a very good day. I didn't know what had gotten into her, but it was illuminating.

After another quick shower and change of clothes, I left her in the room ordering in, heading down to finish my work. But before I got back to my office, I received a call. It was Leo inviting us for late-night drinks. Walking back to the room, I asked Jamie if she wanted to go. I let Leo know we would be there at nine.

Back in my office, I finished the emails and looked at some properties Luder had sent over. Most of the mansions were close by and not too far from the family either. Sitting back in my chair and turning to the window I felt light. I wondered what Jamie would say if I presented her with a mansion just when she was getting used to the den.

She surely wanted a house like any other woman would and the den was no place for a child. After our talk the other night, I asked Luder to assist me with buying a house. Yet, these were all mansions he had sent for consideration. But I guessed it could work. Deciding on one, I told my brother to get the purchase done. I wanted to surprise Jamie with it before the baby came.

I was about to go ask Jamie to join me for an early supper when a note was pushed through under my door. Picking it up, the smell of vanilla and honey filled the air. What was she up to now, I wondered as I opened the note and read it aloud, "Waterfalls and pine trees at dawn, where shall we meet?"

Staring at it, I wondered what Jamie meant. Taking a deep breath, I grinned. This day turned out to be more than I could ever have imagined. Then I remembered how she carried on about the shower and selection of soaps during her first week here. Beaming, I headed to the suite, sure she meant the shower.

Entering the large entrance room, I noticed the bathroom door was half open and heard the water running. The room smelled strongly of vanilla and honey, and I wondered if she washed the floor and walls with body lotion. Grinning at this idea, I locked the door and undressed in a rush before storming into the bathroom naked.

Jamie was standing in the middle of the shower, the water raining down over her. Her hair stuck to her face as she shook her head, biting her lower lip. She looked at me, pointed a finger at me, bent it, and indicated for me to come closer. Feeling my body heating up, I walked over and stepped inside.

Taking Jamie into my arms, I kissed her hard. Her tongue entered my mouth and played inside. As she pulled back, I followed and searched the entrance to her mouth with mine. As my tongue slipped through her soft lips, I felt her sucking it. My blood started to boil like I was floating up the waterfall on the wall behind her.

She reached around and slapped my butt. She had so much spunk in her that I was sure she'd do anything for the rush. Jamie drew a line over my hip as she brought her hand forward and forcefully took hold of my dick. She squeezed tightly as she slowly pulled her hand to her and pushed it back to me.

This woman before me was driving my mind crazy as my cock grew. It felt like it was going to explode if she didn't loosen her grip shortly. Taking hold of her breasts, I gripped her nipples between two fingers and twisted them. Jamie lifted her head and made a purring sound, feeding my sexual desire.

Taking hold of her shoulders, I flipped her around in one swift move. Placing my hand on the back of her neck, I pushed down, bending her over. My cock pushed up between her butt cheeks sending shivers of delight up to my already wild mind.

Slapping her butt with my other hand, I pulled on her hair. Jamie glanced back at me as she split her legs and bent further down. Her butt cheeks lifted into the air as she placed her hands on the floor and her head between her legs. Her pussy flowered between her legs. I had to breathe in deeply as the monster crept out of its dark hole and took control of my body.

Opening her crevasse with my hands, I placed my throbbing dick into her. She was as tight as a vice, filling me with pain and pleasure all at the same time. Pushing further in, I lifted my head and roared. Jamie reached back and took hold of my balls as I moved in and out of her like a bull ride.

She moaned, pulling down on my sacks as I felt her body shaking. She was ready to release. Pushing harder and deeper, the waterfall flowed as the cave closed. Breathing rapidly, I kept going until I exploded. I stood for a second, just holding her hips against my groin. Jamie was gasping for air as she came upright against me.

Turning in my hands, she took my face in hers. "Baby, that was phenomenal," she spoke between breaths before kissing me.

A part of the shower had a seat, and I had to sit down for a moment. It was better than phenomenal, but I couldn't get a word out at the moment. I sat watching her turn in the water and wash her delicious body before she got out and started dressing. Jamie blew me a kiss as she walked to the bedroom to find her shoes.

Once I was ready, I went looking for her. She was seated on the edge of the bed, fastening her last shoe as I entered. Walking over to her, I held out my hand. Standing as she took it, we headed downstairs.

Before leaving, we had a hot drink at the bar and then left to join the family. Jamie looked good in the grey button-up textured fall dress with her black boots and leggings. She was warm and comfortable.

Arriving at Leo's place, I was glad to see that Jamie was less wary and more open with my family. She fell right in place, joining the women in the kitchen.

I met the men in the lounge talking about their latest trips, boats, and cars, but I couldn't keep my eyes off Jamie. My mind wasn't present in the current company; it lingered in the shower. She was like a flower in spring, opening up for the first time. Her amazing strength and beauty were undeniable. She made my heart skip a beat with every laugh.

As I moved closer to pour another drink, I heard her telling Evelina about the man who set her up. She explained how he had set her up and that she was having difficulty finding him. This flared a small fire inside me.

She explained how she wanted to clear her name as I returned to Leo, Luder, and the others. I couldn't help but wonder if Jamie was going to stay or leave once her name was cleared.

In an attempt to keep her safe, I have also been looking for Ben. Jamie and our baby were my first priority, and I didn't want to lose either of them. I was a bit bothered and worried that she might leave thought. I knew this was a possibility but hoped that she would stay.

As the night progressed and the family started leaving, I resolved that I would try and help her more. I pulled Leo to one side and asked if there was any way he could give me access to the needed tools.

Chapter 21 - Jamie

It had been a lovely evening, and I didn't want to go back to the den. But it was getting late, and everyone had their lives. We were some of the last ones to leave. Ashan and I drove back home after thanking Leo and Evelina for a lovely evening.

"Jamie," Ashan said, seemingly a bit distracted. He was glancing from one mirror to the next at short intervals as if looking for something. Before I could reply or ask what was wrong, he continued. "Leo has found a couple of excellent hacking tools and given me access to them. I would like to share this with you as well. That way, you can find the real culprit who messed up your life."

Overwhelmed with emotions, I was speechless. Feeling my eyes starting to burn, I turned away as they teared up. "Thank you," I replied, taking a deep breath and swallowing the lump forming in my throat. Blinking a couple of times, I focused on the buildings passing us by.

"Also," Ashan resumed, giving my leg a quick squeeze. "I've bought a mansion." I heard him taking a deep breath. "I'm sorry for keeping you cooped up at the gambling den. You deserve a proper home." Glancing at him, I saw him smiling at me. "That is if you want one?"

I laughed as overwhelming feelings of gratitude flooded through me. He was finally opening up to me. My heart filled with flutters of joy. He was so kind and caring, A side of him I had barely seen. I was sure that I was falling in love. My mind filled with images of us in a mansion I had not even seen. But my mind could paint pictures of its own.

As we pulled into the parking area, Ashan's phone rang. He took it out of his pocket and mentioned it was his head bodyguard. Getting out of the car, he answered it as he moved to my side and opened the door. Ashan's face fell as I stepped out. The guard was seemingly shouting at him. He was so loud that I could make out some of what he was saying.

He was warning us of trouble at the den. But it was too late as we had already parked and were walking towards the entrance. Ashan dropped his phone. He grabbed my arm and pulled me toward the back of the den. We moved quickly and stayed low as we neared the building.

It was dark at the back. I heard myself swallowing hard as I tried to keep my breathing even. I was afraid of what we might encounter. Pulling his gun, Ashan assisted me to enter through a secret door. He opened what appeared to be a large storage closet on the outside. We stepped into it, and Ashan pushed a button, making the closet turn.

Opening the doors again, we walked into the kitchen. I would never have believed it if I hadn't just seen it. I had passed both the closets inside and outside a million times. I had not even noticed that they had identical items inside.

Entering the darkest corner of the kitchen, we saw that the place was a mess, and we slowly moved into the den. Trays of food lay scattered across the floor. Strolling, I almost slipped. Ashan had to turn and grab me to prevent me from falling.

The floor was sticky and oily. In the darkness, it was hard to see clearly. This was all my fault, I thought. Ashan was only trying to keep me safe, and now look at his place. It was destroyed and it was all because of me. I felt guilty and scared at the same time. I didn't know how I would ever be able to make it up to him.

From the kitchen, we went to the bar area. I moved with Ashan to the booth where we met with the client.

Ashan peeked through the curtains before turning to me. He held my shoulders as he spoke. "Jamie, behind that chair," He pointed to the one he sat on that evening. "There is another passage in the wall like the one in the suite. Take it and go up to the suite."

I saw a glimpse of fear in his eyes as he continued. "Hide in the hidden trap room until the coast is clear, I will come to get you." Ashan pulled me into his arms and kissed me passionately. "Please be safe," he added as he turned back to the lounge and bar area. I was frightened not only for me and the baby but also for Ashan.

What would I do if something happened to him because of me? Where would I go, would his family blame me?

Reaching out for him, I stopped myself from pulling him back. I wanted to go with him but knew that he was right. Getting to the secret room was surely my best option. The attack on the den was my fault, these other groups came looking for me. Ashan wanted me and the baby growing in me safe.

My throat felt like it was closing in on me as my breathing became labored. My heart pounded not only in my chest anymore, but I could also feel it in my feet, my head, and everywhere. It is terror, I told myself, get a grip, you have a baby depending on you. My guilt was eating at my mind. Why had I dragged all of these lovely people into my problems? I should have stayed away. If I hadn't listened to Pedro, none of this would have happened.

Shaking my head I looked back once more before heading up. Ashan was still looking through the curtain, I was sure he was waiting for me to leave before he went out there.

Opening the curtain against the wall behind the chair, I carefully took the now narrow passage. Even though I had not taken this one before, I was sure it had shrunk. Grinning at myself as I knew I had grown, I exited into Ashan's office. My heart was racing as there were gunshots from downstairs.

Instinctively, I wanted to run down and make sure Ashan was safe. The office door was closed, but I could hear voices coming from outside. Breathing slowly and softly, I quickly entered the other passage and headed up to the suite.

Stepping out of the passage, I saw our suite was empty. The bedroom and bathroom doors were open. Clothing and other items decorated the floor, and I knew whoever was out there had already been in there.

Moving toward the bedroom, I thought of rather staying in there as it would be more comfortable. But what if they came back or if a stray bullet came through the walls? Deciding against it, I crept to the door and peeked out. The hallway was quiet; it was kind of creepy, and I saw no one out there.

It was usually lit up and had people moving this way and that at all times. Now, it was dimly lit and was empty of any life.

Closing the door quietly again, I leaned against it, trying to relax my breathing. I hurried to the hidden trap door in the wall but noticed the computer also lying on the floor. Maybe they weren't looking for me, it could be that whoever started this fight was after the Morozov family.

There were surely turf wars and such things. Rubbing my cheek, I felt it was cold. Deciding that the mess outside wasn't about me, I decided to change into something warmer first. I didn't dare get sick while I was pregnant, I thought as I entered the bathroom. Plus, I would still hide as Ashan had asked but I would do it once I was warmer.

Sifting through the mess, I finally found a warm tracksuit I could change into. Once I felt warmer and comfortable, I moved back to the hidden compartment in the wall.

Pulling open the life-size mirror that hid the secret room, I gasped. Someone was already inside. I stepped back and tried to focus on the dark figure sitting in the chair. But before I could see who it was, I felt an immense pain traveling through my head. Grabbing my head, I tried to turn around. My eyes teared up, and my vision blurred as I felt my legs give way.

The floor was coming at me very quickly. Leaving my pounding head, I pushed my hands out, stopping my head just in time before knocking it against the floor. I slammed into the ground hard, though. My lungs felt as if they had been crushed as I exhaled sharply. Pushing up, I tried to look around but only saw darkness as I lost consciousness.

Chapter 22 - Ashan

With Jamie on her way up and safe, I peeked out of the booth. Dialing Luder, I asked for backup quickly, letting him know what was happening even though I wasn't too sure myself. Luder would let the rest know and assured me his men were already on their way.

Most of the tables were lying on their sides. The bar area and counter displayed broken bottles, and puddles of liquid and glass everywhere. As I moved out of the booth and went closer, I noticed two guards lying by the entrance.

Staying hunched over, I moved to their side. "Are you okay?" I whispered to Frank as he was the one sitting against the table. He was holding his side and grunted as he nodded before pointing to the other guard lying face down. Moving closer, I saw he was lying in a pool of blood.

Slowly peeking around the doorway out at the entrance hall, I felt for a pulse. Sighing, I shook my head, glancing back at Frank. "He didn't make it," I whispered. Staying low, I moved back to Frank. "Where's everyone else, and what the hell happened here?" I asked, checking his wound.

"I'm not sure," he replied. "I was doing my normal rounds when I heard the shots echoing through the entrance hall. I pulled my gun and came this way hoping to stop whoever was bragging in." His face was white from blood loss. Moving his hands away only a tad, I saw the blood was seeping through his fingers. Picking up one of the tablecloths that lay close by, I gave it a good shake before making it into a ball. I placed it over the hole in his side.

"Hold it tight, help is on the way," I said as I started to move towards the entranceway. Glancing around the room, I tried to see if the bodies scattered towards the door or those by the stairs were any of mine. Some were my men, but only a couple. Most of them were seemingly from other groups I didn't recognize. It looked like they were all dead, as no one moved a muscle. Stepping carefully over them, I headed to the stairs.

As I moved up the stairs, I heard a couple of gunshots. They had not left, I thought, aiming my guns out in front of me. I was sure that these men were from different mafia groups as they wore different suits. It was an unspoken policy between the Bratva groups, a way for us to know the company we keep.

I thought these had to be from some of the groups that were looking for Jamie. Most looked as if they were part of smaller groups. Many of their outfits or tattoos I had never seen before. I was about to step out on the first-floor landing when I felt a hand closing around my ankle. Glancing down, I looked into a smashed face. The guy was half-dead and stared at me with one bloodied eye barely still in its socket.

Shooting him wasn't an option, as I would alert the remaining intruders of my presence. Pulling my foot free, I pushed him down the stairs. He rolled a couple of times making barely audible gurgling sounds as he went. Coming to rest a few steps down he tried turning his head my way but couldn't.

With no time to waste, I stepped onto the landing and surveyed the area. In the distance, I heard some more shots and someone screaming. Heading to my office, I found some more of my injured men in the hall. After checking and assisting them as best I could, I continued on my path.

The office door was open, so I moved slowly so as to not make any noise. Peeking in I saw no one inside, but it was trashed. Books and papers lay scattered over the desk and floor. All the drawers and cupboards were open and most of their contents had been emptied to the floor with the papers.

Turning in a slow circle, I breathed in and out to control my raging anger. The building appeared quiet now. Listening, I heard nothing, not even voices or footsteps.

What were they seeking I wondered. There was nothing of value or importance here. Everything gets stored at a warehouse. It made no sense to go through everything if they were looking for Jamie. But, what were they seeking if they weren't looking for her?

Hearing whispers in the hall, I moved to stand behind the door. I was ready with my guns raised. Once the voices were right outside, I stepped out into the hall, pushing my guns out before me, ready to shoot.

"Whoa, brother," Luder shouted. "It's us, we're here to help." He had his hands raised into the air.

Relief washed over me, seeing the family filling the hall. "What happened?" Leo and Evelina asked simultaneously.

"I think they were looking for Jamie," I replied shaking my head as I looked back at the mess in my office.

"This is war," Luder added angrily, placing his hands on his hips. "My men have started to clear the bottom floor, and Leo sent his men up to the top."

"Whoever they are. They won't get away with it, we will find them and deal with them appropriately," Evelina spat, pulling her radio up to her mouth. Pressing the button, she gave the remaining men waiting outside their orders. "Round them up, boys, the second floor is yours."

"You said they were looking for Jamie?" Leo asked, raising his eyebrows as she scanned the hall. "Where is she?"

"Jamie," I breathed out as I remembered I sent her up to hide. Turning on my heels, I dashed down the passage and through the suite door. I yanked open the hidden one to the side. My heart sank as I stared blankly into the emptiness before me.

"No, no, no," I yelled as Luder entered the room behind me.

Turning to him, I noticed a piece of paper on the floor where he was standing. Picking it up from the floor, I unfolded it. The life drained out of me as I read it out loud.

"We have her, if you want her back, wait for our call, we'll be in touch."

I sank to my knees, my body weak, tapped of all life. Holding the dirty piece of paper, my hand shook as the room appeared to swirl and close in on me. I struggled to breathe, my eyes stung, and my head felt like it was swelling.

"They have taken Jamie. How could this have happened?" I whispered, glancing up at Luder. An immense pain filled my chest.

"Breathe, calm down, we will find her," Luder said holding out his hand.

Allowing my rage to take over, I slapped my cheeks. Jamie needed me, and I had no time to wallow. Standing up I nodded at him before turning and storming out of the room. Luder followed close on my heels. We found Leo, Evelina, and the others downstairs.

They have rounded up all the enemy Bratva in the lounge area. Storming in I headed to the first guy I saw. Picking him up by the throat, I slammed him into the wall as I screamed at him. "Where is she? If you don't tell me, I'll kill you! Where is Jamie?"

The young man's eyes widened; he gasped for air as I forcefully kept slamming him into the wall.

Feeling a hand on my shoulder, I glanced around but didn't let go of the man.

"Ashan," Leo said pulling on my arm. "Let him go before you do kill him. We have to handle this smartly. Tell us what happened from the start and maybe we can help."

I handed him the note to as I slowly dropped the young man back down. Turning, I noticed everyone was looking at me.

"I," I started saying but didn't know what to say. My heart was racing and my mind pounding just thinking of what they might do to Jamie.

Evelina stepped up to me taking hold of my shoulders as she spoke. "Leave finding her to Leo and me, okay? We will get her back."

All I could do was nod. Staring at the blood on my hands, I went back to our suite and got cleaned up. Rinsing my face, I stared at my reflection in the mirror. "It will be fine; you will get her; no harm will come to her. You got this." I told the enraged bull staring back at me.

Once I felt calmer, I headed back down to aid Luder. We questioned everyone and searched for a connection between them.

While we were doing that, Leo and Evelina put their skills together to work on one last hacking project. Evelina had given it up years ago, but to get Jamie back, she would aid Leo. They traced Jamie's hack and compiled a list of groups that were exposed after she infiltrated the networks.

Comparing their list to the one Luder and I made, we checked to see which ones had colluded together and who wasn't part of the original attack. Everyone had ideas of how to proceed. Listening to the family, it struck me. I knew how we would handle this.

After a round of interrogation of certain suspects downstairs, I found the link, and we knew who had taken her.

CHAPTER 23 - JAMIE

My head was pounding, everything was stiff. It felt like I had been run over and then dragged behind an eighteen-wheeler. I tried moving but couldn't do that either. Trying to open my eyes, I had to flutter them a bit before they opened. The light was extremely bright, burning my eyes. But I had to know where I was.

As my vision settled, metal walls and brick flooring came into view, it reminded me of a warehouse. Surveying the area around me, I realized I was indeed in a warehouse.

It wasn't the one I had seen before when Pedro rescued me, as there were no rooms. In the furthest corner, there appeared to be some crates and barrels, though. But other than that, the entire area I could see was bare. Fear set in as I searched for those who had captured me.

Straining my neck left and right, I tried to see as far back as I could. I was sure it must have been one of the Bratva groups I was hiding from that captured me. I was terrified that I would be tortured for information.

Yet, the place appeared quite deserted. There were no guards or men with weapons as expected when one thinks of Bratva. I couldn't see torture equipment or anything else that was dangerous, the place was empty. I wondered how they intended to extract the information if they weren't going to use torture.

At least I wasn't gagged, I thought. The ropes around my wrists and ankles were a bit tight and were cutting into my skin. The ones around my wrists were average-looking. I couldn't see any blood but felt my skin burning under the pressure. I couldn't see the ones around my legs but was sure they were the same. They also had pressure on but felt slightly looser as My ankles didn't burn.

Glancing around, I didn't bother to scream, I felt sure it wouldn't be of any use, and that was why I wasn't gagged. I was sure the warehouse was isolated, and no one would be around if it was still night. With no windows, and not knowing how long I'd been out, I wasn't sure if it was still night or if the day had sauntered in yet. I scanned the area with as much focus as I could muster, trying to figure out if there was any way I could escape while I was still alone.

Somewhere behind me, I heard a door creaking open and some voices. Listening carefully as I sat dead still, I could make out only two voices. One was a man, but the other was undoubtedly a woman. Both voices sounded somewhat familiar. I tried to think where I knew them from, yet I couldn't place them. Thinking made my headache more intense. Shaking my head softly, I let go of my thoughts.

Sitting still, I waited for the voices to come closer. I realized I knew the man, hearing them whispering close behind me. "Pedro," I asked warily. "Pedro, is that you?"

"Well, well, well, look who's woken up." The woman said as she came into view. "Look, little Miss Perfect is awake, Pedro."

"Ana," I breathed out, astonished as she came to stand before me. Then I saw Pedro joining her. My mind whirled as I tried to formulate the facts of the situation. I felt betrayed, how could these two people who knew me and knew Ashan very well, do such a thing to us?

Ana was dressed all in black, and I now understood my memory of the mirror room. It was her hiding in there. That meant that Pedro was the one who had hit me on the head.

"What's going on here, let me go," I added, looking from him to her and back at him. "Ashan's going to find me, and you're going to pay. But, if you let me go now, we can forget that it ever happened, okay?"

His face was still bruised from the beating Ashan had given him, and he had a scar just above one eye. "I'm so sorry for what happened," I said sincerely. "But this. Keeping me captured is a bad idea."

"I'm sure you are very sorry, but sorry doesn't fix it, sweetie," Pedro replied. I could hear resentment in his voice, accompanied by anger and hate. I couldn't believe my ears; Pedro was blaming me. It was his own doing that got him a beating.

Giggling, I shook my head at the odd pair, feeling less threatened. "You know Ashan's going to find me, and this time he's going to kill you," I said as they stared at me in disbelief.

Ana made a growling sound before speaking. "You don't belong with him, and he will see that once you're out of the picture. I'll be ready when he needs comforting after your demise."

"It was you, you told them where to find me," I spat at Ana angrily. "You're working with the enemy?"

Ana bared her teeth at me, hissing like the snake she was. "They thought they would get you and make you pay for what you've done. But we got to you first, and you will never see the light of day again." Ana said, pulling out a gun and aiming it at me.

Pedro's eyes widened, seeing the gun. "Whoa, stop, Ana, this wasn't the plan or deal we had. Remember, we'd only keep her here until she's been auctioned off to this highest bidder." He said, pulling carefully at her arm.

"No, Pedro," Ana screamed at him. Her face turned red as anger and hate surged through her." She's not worth the money or the trouble. She stole Ashan from me," she glared at me, her loathing clearly showing as she spoke. "For that, she needs to pay, and she will, with her life."

As they argued, I slowly worked at the ropes. One of the guards I befriended had shown me how to get out of bounds should I ever get captured. At the time, I still joked with him that it was something I would never need. But now I was extremely grateful that he insisted, and I know now. It was a lot harder, but I was confident I would get out of them if I had enough time.

Twisting and turning my hands slowly, I managed to move the knot. Little by little, it shifted from the bottom to the side of my hands. Having the knot closer, I managed to get a nail into it. Slowly I worked at it until I managed to put a finger into the loops. I loosened it with my finger while keeping an eye on my two abductors. If they saw I was trying to escape, who knew what would happen?

They were still deep in their argument, both pulling at the gun. It moved left and right as they fought about my fate. Pulling my one hand free, I untied my other one slowly, glad it was rope and not straps or something like that.

I took a deep breath. It was just my feet; I still had to free myself. I sat still for a second, breathing in deeply. Once I was sure they wouldn't notice, I leaned over and untied my legs. I felt sure Ana had tied me up as the knots were easy to loosen.

Glancing back around the side of the chair, I noticed the door was quite a way. The two were still arguing. They had moved a couple of feet back from me during their struggle, and I knew I had to try. Sliding off the chair and watching them I turned to the door. Jumping to my feet I sprinted for the door. My head pounded, and I still felt a little dizzy, but my legs worked just fine.

"She's getting away," I heard Ana screaming. I didn't dare look back and kept my focus on getting to the door. I hadn't even considered that it could be locked. Running towards it, I could only hope that it wasn't locked.

As I reached out to grab the handle, I heard a loud thump and felt a hand closing around my ankle. Falling forward with my throat closing and my heart ripping through my ribs, I tried to stop my fall with my hands. Pain shot up my arms as I collided with the floor.

Glancing around, I saw Pedro jump at me, and he lay on the floor behind me. Turning to my back, I kicked at his hands and tried to move out of his grip. Looking up, I saw Ana standing behind him with the gun pointed straight at my head. I stopped moving as Ana walked closer. She struck me on the side of my head with the gun. "That wasn't nice," she spat at me.

Pedro had risen to his feet. He came around and pulled me up from behind. I was so close; I would have taken just a couple more steps and been free. Lowering my head, I felt the tears welling up.

"No running," Pedro uttered as he dragged me back to the chair. After tying up again, he turned to Ana as he spoke. "No damaging the merchandise, we need her alive and intact. That was the deal. Plus, the first bidders will be here in about an hour."

"No, no, no," Ana replied, pacing up and down. "We don't need money." She screamed, slamming her foot to the floor, and flinging her arms down. She stopped and turned to me, lifting the gun again. "She has to die," she continued through clenched teeth. Her eyes were wild, and she looked as if she belonged in an asylum.

Terror flooded my body as I realized this day might not end too well. If Pedro couldn't keep her in line, I might actually die here. I considered sharing the fact that I was pregnant but didn't know if that would make a difference to either of them.

Once again Pedro interrupted. "Ana, think about what you're saying. You want those groups to come after us?" I understood what he meant, and it made sense. If they killed me, they had no use and would surely be taken out for the betrayal.

Yet, Ana was so filled with hate that she couldn't see it, and I knew if I informed them of the baby, she wouldn't think twice about killing me. I watched in horror as Pedro tried to take the gun, but Ana just wouldn't let go. As they struggled a shot rang through the air. I felt a sting in my left arm. Looking down I saw the bright red liquid slowly moving down my arm.

My sleeve was torn, but it didn't look like the bullet had penetrated my arm. The pain was severe, but the heat was worse. It felt like someone had inserted a lump of burning coal into my arm. Biting down on my lower lip, I kept my scream inside, but I couldn't keep my body from shaking.

"What the fuck, Ana. Look what you've done now," Pedro shouted as he shoved Ana back. She went sprawling to the floor and lost her grip on the gun. I watched as the gun slid across the floor just out of her reach. Ana turned to her hands and knees, crawling towards the gun.

Pedro tried to move past her to pick it up when Ana grabbed his legs, sending him flying to the floor. They reached the gun at the same time and were rolling around fighting for control. I couldn't watch anymore as fear of another shot going off and hitting me again settled in.

My arms and legs tingled as the blood in my veins seemed to turn to ice. Sweat broke out all over my body. It started running down my face stinging my eyes, and I couldn't even wipe it away.

Then, their struggle was abruptly interrupted as I heard the door open with a loud banging. Glancing around frantically as I expected the room to fill with Bratva, I noticed I knew some of the men quickly filling the warehouse.

Seconds later, Ashan, his brother, all the cousins, and Ashan's men surrounded me. Ana and Pedro scrambled to their feet and tried to flee but Ashan's men caught them. I breathed out hard as relief washed over me. He had found me I thought, trying to calm my racing heart.

I instantly felt like the world had been removed from my shoulders as tears streamed down my face. But they were tears of joy and no longer due to fear. Ashan stood before me facing Ana and Pedro. He was my knight in shining armor. With the feelings of relaxation knowing it was over, came a sense of gratitude.

His presence flooded the room with a noticeable strength and calmness I couldn't even begin to describe.

Chapter 24 - Ashan

"Stop," I screamed as we barged into the warehouse. After hours of scouring the internet and making calls, we finally found out who had captured Jamie. As we entered, I saw Ana and Pedro arguing. They were rolling around on the floor. Jamie sat tied to a chair in the middle of the warehouse.

Seeing her alive, I felt my rage calming. I wanted to run to her and take her into my arms, but we had to secure the situation first. She beamed at me, and a ray of sunshine flooded my heart as it skipped a beat. Even in all this turmoil she shone, she was the most beautiful woman I had ever known.

The two jumped to their feet and tried to run as we filled the room, but my guards caught them. Ana went down to the floor again as she tried to escape but seemingly couldn't find her feet. Pedro stopped and pulled at her to assist, but it was in vain. My men got to them before they could move. They dragged Ana to her feet fighting and screaming, she was even kicking at them.

Pedro just complied, he lowered his head and just stood there. "Stop, Ana," I yelled at her. "Don't you two even try running! We know who you got into bed with to pull this off, but your plans won't work."

Walking to Jamie, I noticed the blood on her arm. Kneeling before her as I untied her, I spoke gently. "Jamie, I'm so sorry. Are you okay?"

She flung her arms around my neck, burying her head in me. "Thank you," she whispered. I filled with warmth as I rose holding her tightly.

Relief washed over me having her in my arms, even if it was only for a second or two.

Letting go, I checked her arm, noting it was only a scrape. I hugged her again. She was the best thing that had ever happened in my life, and I wouldn't let anything happen to her or our child.

I wished Evelina had come with us. She would know better about treating wounds, but she had to stay behind. She was back at the den discussing an alliance with the groups that weren't part of this attack. We had to be sure that something like this wouldn't be possible moving forward. Our allies would become Jamie's allies, and this would offer her more protection.

Leo took a look at Jamie's arm. "She'll be okay, we'll get the doctor in as soon as we get back," he said.

"This isn't over," Ana screamed. Turning as the guards walked with her past us Jamie let go of me and stepped up to Ana.

Jamie was angry. Who could blame her? "Why, Ana, why do you want me dead?" Jamie inquired. I shared her pain and knew she only wanted answers. It didn't make any sense to me either.

Ana started shaking, she twisted and turned violently. The guards struggled to hold her, and she managed to pull free of the grip they had on her. She grabbed Jamie, wrenched her around, and out of nowhere, she pulled a gun and held it to Jamie's head. I felt my heart being ripped from my chest and stood for a minute frozen in fear. Moving forward very slowly, I realized we needed to tread carefully.

"Ana," I heard Pedro speaking from behind me. "Please, don't do this. Ashan will forgive us for our poor judgment." He continued as I stepped back and turned sideways to see him. "You will, won't you, Ashan."

Before I could get a word out, the loud boom of a gunshot echoed through the open warehouse. Pedro sank to the ground, clutching his chest as his blood flowed through his hands out of the bullet hole. He lay groaning as some of my men rushed over to help him.

Looking back at Ana, she appeared wild and out of control. Her eyes were wide as she shook her head very faintly. She was aiming the gun left and right as she screamed. "Back off, all of you or I'll shoot Jamie. Back off I said, back off!"

My men moved back a tad, but they all had their guns pointed at her. Ana placed the gun to Jamie's head again as she took a step back pulling Jamie with her.

I slowly walked toward them, lifting my hands up into the air before me. I lowered my voice and spoke softly. "Ana, please talk to me, tell me what you want. Why are we here?"

Ana grinned at me angrily. "This is all you're doing," she spat at me. She ground the gun against Jamie's head as she continued. "Stop Ashan, what do you think you're doing? Don't come closer, I'll shoot."

I stopped moving and took a couple of deep breaths. Alarms shot through me as I noticed Ana looked a bit crazy not just wild. I didn't want Jamie to get hurt. "Okay, then explain to me what's going on?" I asked calmly, hoping to defuse the situation without anyone else getting hurt.

"Once she came along," Ana spat, tapping the gun tip against Jamie's head. "You discarded me like an old rag. You threw me away like all the years together meant nothing." Ana's eyes filled with tears as she spoke. Her voice started breaking and she swallowed a couple of times hard holding back the sobs. "I gave you everything." She said, glancing at her feet.

Ana shook her head as she looked me in the eyes. "Wasn't what we had special? Didn't it mean anything to you?" She was screaming again. Ana was losing control, and I knew I had to get Jamie out of her grip.

My heart was racing a thousand miles, my ribs felt bruised as it pounded in my chest, and I felt sweat running down my back. "Ana, please, haven't I been good to you all the years? I only let you go after you manipulated me."

Ana shook her head, she pointed the gun at me, then back to Jamie. Then to me and again back to Jamie as she started rambling. "No, no, no. I gave you everything."

At that moment, I realized I would have to swallow my pride to keep her calm. "Okay, okay, Ana," I said as calmly as I could muster. "I'm very sorry if I hurt you. I promise you it wasn't intentional."

Slowly stepping forward, I hoped to get close enough to get Jamie away from her. "I really didn't mean to hurt you or offend you in any way. If I wronged you, I ask your forgiveness. Please, Ana."

Ana stared blankly at me for a moment. Jamie noticed Ana was distracted by me. She pulled her arm forward and elbowed Ana in the ribs. Ana exhaled sharply letting go of her grip. Jamie darted towards me, but I saw Ana regaining herself and reacting quickly.

She lifted the gun aiming at Jamie, but I couldn't let her shoot, Jamie. As she squeezed the trigger, I jumped, pushing Jamie out of the way. The bullet bore through the upper right side of my chest just below my shoulder.

It was luckily a small gun, but the Smith & Wesson M2 packed a hard punch, nonetheless. I grabbed my shoulder and staggered backward a couple of steps. Feeling Jamie behind me, I tried to stay on my feet. I didn't want to push her over or fall on top of her. My chest was burning, and a hot, sticky liquid flowed through my fingers.

Looking down, I saw my hand covered in red as the blood forced its way through my fingers. I was relieved to know I had taken the bullet, which meant Jamie was safe. Even though I was shot, I was glad it was me, and Jamie was safe.

Glancing at Ana, her mouth hung open, and her eyes were shocked. Her eyes followed me as I fell on my knees, trying not to tip over. She hadn't intended on shooting me and her disbelief was evident. Dropping the gun, her hands shot up to her open mouth, covering it as she started screaming.

My guards moved in, kicked the gun away, and dragged her away. I could hear her screaming hysterically as they moved her out of the warehouse. I breathed out deeply as my body fell to the floor.

Staring up at the ceiling, I noticed Jamie kneeling next to me. She had taken off her jacket and balled it up. Taking away my hand she placed it on the wound and applied pressure. Luder had called our surgeon. They weren't going to move me. He went outside to wait for him to arrive. I smiled at Jamie, noticing the tears running down her face. "It's going to be fine. Please don't cry." I said softly reaching up and caressing her cheek.

The doctor worked quickly to remove the bullet and patch me up. He ordered me to stay in bed for at least a week and give my shoulder six to twelve weeks to heal. As soon as my arm was bandaged, we could all go back to the den.

Leo and Luder stayed behind to clean up and make sure that there were no traces of us ever being there. We weren't sure who the owner of the warehouse was and didn't want repercussions.

Evelina assisted Jamie in getting me settled. Jamie would learn to do the day-to-day checks with assistance from Frank and Cleo. Luder and Evelina also offered to stay and assist with the gambling den. I was still a bit heartbroken about all the destruction, but I was overjoyed that everything turned out okay and Jamie was safe.

With all the damage to the den, it would be a couple of weeks before we could open again but I had Jamie by my side. The first week I allowed her to treat me and assist with the daily tasks. She made sure everything went smoothly everyday and I couldn't be more grateful.

Having her assist in washing me was one of the many pleasures of being injured. Everyday I grew in strenght and desire for her. By the end of the second week I couldn't contain my lust anymore. As we crawled into bed and Jamie lay her head on my chest I whispered in her ear.

"Jamie, I want you."

Turning her head up to me, she placed a warm kiss on my cheek as she spoke. "Sleep Ashan, not yet."

"I'm ready, I promise." I responded feeling my dick coming to life.

She softly rubbed up and down my chest. "Let's give it another day or so. I'm a bit worn tonight."

Accepting her reply, I hugged her tightly and allowed sleep to take me.

Jamie was already up when I woke. I heard the shower running; glancing over, I noticed the door was only halfway closed. As I got up, the water stopped. "Jamie, you done already," I called out as I rolled out of bed and stood up, heading to the bathroom. I had hoped to catch her in the shower.

"You know how amazing you are?" I added as I pushed the door open. It was empty; I turned and peeked back into the room. But she wasn't there. Opening the door to the entrance room, I wondered where she could have gone so quickly. Getting undressed, I wondered if I just imagined the water running.

She was amazing, and I wanted her to know that. With all she had on her plate, all that had passed, she stood strong. I decided to take a shower first and then go looking for her. I was ready to retake my morning routine. Once it was done, I could take her out a bit. Stepping into the shower, I grinned at myself as my mind wandered to the variety of lingerie I saw in one of the shops the other day.

After a quick hot shower, with a towel around my waist, I opened the walk-in closet to grab some clothes. As I opened the door, I almost had a heart attack as my mind was still on images of her in nothing but sexy undergarments.

Seated on the floor of the closet was Jamie in nothing but my suit jacket. She was smiling seductively at me. "You looking for clothes or for me?" she asked softly as she licked her lips.

"Well," I replied. "I'm not too sure anymore." Stepping closer, I pulled Jamie to her feet, placing my hands on her hips.

Her hands came to rest on my wet chest. Moving her fingertips over my nipples stirred the storm I suddenly felt rising within. Kissing her forehead, I closed my eyes. Her sweet smell of honey and vanilla penetrated my senses. Feeling her hot breath on my chest as she came closer and licked my nipples made me shudder.

Once again, she was blowing my mind. I had no idea she would be ready after putting me down last night, but I wouldn't complain. Tilting my head back, I breathed in sharply as I felt her biting my nipples softly. There was a wild beast inside me that wanted to throw her to the floor and penetrate her with my stiffened dick.

Controlling the beast, I allowed her to explore my godly figure. Jamie kissed my neck and chest. I was sure that, somehow, I was still dreaming as her hands trailed down the center of my body toward my pumping dick. After she loosened the towel, allowing it to drop to the floor, she continued her path down my body. Her fingers left a burning trail of delight as she cupped my balls.

Stretching backward, I opened my legs, allowing her easier access to my precious jewels. I felt her fingers trailing back to the base of my dick, her touch so tender I shivered. Closing her hand around my shaft, she pulled forward and then pushed back with some force. I wanted to buck from the bliss she streamed through me as I tried to catch my breath.

Pushing out my chest, I stayed upright as she draped my chest and stomach in tender love bites. As she moved further down, going down on her knees before me, I couldn't resist pushing my fingers into her silky strands, grabbing hold of her head.

Jamie kissed the head of the beast before placing the tip into her warm, wet mouth. I growled as my body shook, delighted by her soft sucking. Moving her closed hand up and down the shaft of my dick, she took turns licking and sucking the tip. I was truly stunned by her boldness as I felt my body reacting with trebles like the waves of the ocean growing. Opening my mouth, I allowed my moans to fill the room as she made me cum in her mouth.

Pulling back, I bent forward and lifted Jamie into my arms. Our lips met with warmth and passion as she wrapped her legs around my waist. I felt a slight pulling in my chest but feeling my dick pumping between her legs, I pushed the pain from my mind. Moving forward, I pinned her to the wall.

Jamie gasped as I kissed her fiercely. She undid the button of my jacket, allowing it to open for easy access to the rest of her. Moving down her neck to her breasts, I wanted as much of her as I could get. Sucking on her breasts, I felt her body shiver as I pushed my dick into her welcoming garden.

There was no stopping as my mind left my body, and my animal instinct took over. Our body's slipped from the sweet sweat as I held her ass, driving my dick harder into her. Jamie breathed warmly over my shoulder before burying her face in my neck.

"Fuck me, baby," she whispered between jagged gasps for air. Exhilarated by her words, I held tight as I turned with her. I lay her down on the long ottoman standing in the middle of the room. Going down on my knees, I pulled her legs up to my chest. Jamie placed her feet over my shoulders and smiled at me.

Gripping her legs, I pulled her down to the edge and pushed my dick further into her. Jamie moaned as I moved in and out. My body started to shake with each move, and I felt her pussy tightening. Lifting my face to the ceiling, I growled as I filled her. Jamie panted before she let out a scream, which I was sure could be heard from miles away as she came.

Collapsing my head onto her stomach, she stroked my hair. We were dripping with sweat, but I didn't mind. Glancing up at her, I beamed as I stood and picked her up again.

"Now, this was fun, wasn't it?" I breathed out as I stepped into the shower with Jamie in my arms.

She nodded but looked tired. "Are you okay?" I asked as I lowered her.

"Yes, I am," she replied, turning to me and throwing her arms around my neck. "Thank you," she added, kissing my cheek softly.

My face tightened as my smile stretched across it from ear to ear. Taking a sponge, I lathered her in soap. Jamie stood, allowing me to wash her from head to toe. My mind was blown, but I had never felt as relaxed as I had been then. She was the one, I thought as we rinsed the soap from our bodies.

Together we went through the daily checks and emails before having a calming meal on the upper deck. At almost fife months pregnant her belly had risen nicely. I admired her strength and resolve, she was one of a kind and in that moment I knew I would hold on for life.

CHAPTER 25 - JAMIE

It had been about three weeks since the incident. The den was almost ready to re-open, and Ashan was back to his stubborn self. The first week went surprisingly well. He allowed me to do most things for him and stayed in bed.

But after the second week, he insisted on doing his own things, and they all had to be done a certain way. He was driving me insane; I was about ready to climb the walls. I had taken up painting classes just to have a couple of hours to myself every day.

During the three weeks, Evelina and Leo also assisted me in finding Ben. During our search for Ben, Evelina introduced me to an underground mafia group from NY. They were also a smaller group but potent. Without them, I would never have found Ben.

Leo and Evelina's men infiltrated Ben's home and captured him. It took a couple of days to break him though, but we eventually got the information out of him. Ben confessed that he was working for a small mafia group. They were trying to cause issues between the bigger groups.

With the information I provided, they hoped to make the bigger groups fight against each other. Once most of them were taken out, they could make a name and rise. This, however, didn't happen as I didn't hand over what he wanted. He eventually confessed to setting me up and agreed to clear my name.

The next week was up and down as Ben worked with Evelina to set things straight. Having cleared the air eventually felt good. I could once again breathe without having to look over my shoulder. I could lead a normal life with Ashan after all.

After we cleared my name, I contacted the ungodly brothers again to thank them for everything. I also struck a deal with them for future trade. We gave them both Pedro and Ana to work off the debt they owed us. They had caused a lot of trouble and had to pay for it. The brothers were in need of hands and were grateful for two new slaves.

They were my first secure and I felt good. Everyone was pleased and I was now also seen as an invaluable member of the Morozov family. With their help, we were able to shut down all threats. The next couple of weeks were filled with meetings establishing stronger ties with our allies.

The work on the gambling den took a bit longer than expected. Instead of four weeks, we were now at eight weeks but finally ready. After the re-opening of the gambling den and the final signatures on the mansion, we moved in. At first, the three-story mansion seemed a bit much for me. But after a couple of days were settled nicely.

It wasn't as big as Leo's place but had more than enough house and yard. The house was nestled in one corner of the yard. Coming in through the gate, it almost seemed like half of the yard was made up of parking. That wasn't the case, it only looked that way as the yard fell on a hill.

Coming in by the enormous gates, you could only see half of the house. The parking area stretched wide and was met by a lush green lawn that flowed up to the house. There were two small fountains where a footpath started in the middle of the lawn heading up to the house. The sides of the gravel-filled footpath were decorated by bedding filled with a variety of colorful flowers.

It wasn't as elaborate as Leo's, but it was stunning and perfect for us. The house was an older structure boasting a tinge of Victorian style. It had large windows with wooden frames and the most amazing patterns. I fell in love with it from the moment I saw it first.

Entering the house, you walked into a large entrance hall that led out to the kitchen, lounge, and dining room. From the kitchen were steps going up to the other two floors. On the second floor were three bedrooms and a study. The top floor held the most. It only had one bedroom and provided a study, library, office, and entertainment area.

I never truly understood why people had inside entertainment areas if they also had outside ones. We decided to change it into a playroom for the kids and the office would move to the second floor so we could have another bedroom upstairs. But all of this would come in time.

Outside behind the house was a reasonably large patio with enough space for about ten tables with chairs. It had a BBQ and bar area as well and led further down to the pool area. The place was breathtaking and more than I ever dreamed of.

To the side of the house, we also discovered an enclosed jacuzzi. It had a door leading into the kitchen and one leading out toward the patio. It was almost like a small entertainment area on its own with a built-in bar and enough space to host about ten people.

We will keep this space for ourselves for now. The jacuzzi had seating right around and looked very cozy. We couldn't wait to try it, yet, we still had so much to do there was just never time.

Ashan organized a family gathering for the following weekend. I was excited to assist with the last plans for the get-together as it kept me busy. Now that the den was operating fully again, I had a lot more time.

Once everything was set for Saturday, Ashan arranged with a local contractor to start planning the changes we wanted done on the house. The week passed by quicker than expected, and before I knew it, Saturday had arrived.

I woke before dawn. Crawling out of bed, I stepped outside so I didn't wake Ashan. Standing on our bedroom balcony, I could see and smell the ocean. The cool morning breeze kissed my skin, sending a shiver down my spine. I was so entranced by the picture before me that I jumped when Ashan spoke behind me.

"What are you doing out here so early?" Ashan held out my robe as he walked closer. Smiling, I turned so he could throw it over my shoulders. He draped it over me and pulled me into his warm embrace. "Good morning, love," he added as he kissed my cheek.

We stood watching the sun light up the world as it rose higher, waking up nature. "Are you ready for the day?" I asked as I turned out of his arms and headed back in.

"Yes, are you?" Ashan replied following me in. "It's going to be good to see everyone together again." He added, pulling me in and kissing me hard. "Thank you for helping with everything; I am sure it is going to be a great evening."

After taking a quick shower, we got dressed. As always, Ashan wore jeans, a casual button-up shirt, and his white sneakers. At eight months pregnant, there was no clothing to hide my bump anymore. After standing before my selection of dresses, I finally decided on one. Putting on the elegant peach-colored off-shoulder Tulle dress with slits up the sides, I took out a pair of sandals.

My feet had been killing me this week, and there was just no way I was wearing heels. I applied a light shade of makeup and pinned up my hair before joining Ashan in the kitchen.

We had a quick breakfast before the florists, caterers, and staff arrived. By midday, the décor had been done, and the place looked fit for a king and queen.

The caterers had delivered all the food by four, and we were set. Roman, Karine, Leo, Samantha, and Evelina were the first ones to arrive. They pulled in as if they were traveling together. We had barely shown them the house and had just sat down outside when the rest started streaming in.

Most of the men were quite content with having drinks outside while I took the women through the house. Luder and Skyler had been here twice this week, so they also waited outside with Ashan and the others.

Returning to the patio, I noticed some of the tables had been moved into a circle. Karine, Sam, and Skyler sat waiting for us to join them. They sat where an eye could be kept on the little ones exploring the back garden.

Grabbing a round of drinks from the bar, I gave Ashan a quick kiss and sat down with them. We had barely started when Ashan pinged a fork against his glass drawing everyone's attention. I had not been sure why he wanted a gathering so soon at our house but seeing him step forward, I knew that something big was about to happen.

Ashan cleared his throat before speaking. "First, let me just thank you all for coming." There was a string of "always, any time, thanks for the invite, sure thing," and more making the rounds as most of the men replied to him. He waited for everyone to quiet down before continuing.

"You all know we have been through some rough waters these last months, and I am grateful to each and everyone who assisted." Another murmur went through, and Ashan waited again. It was kind of strange to see him waiting patiently as they kept giving their replies.

"Please, you do not need to answer," Ashan said as silence filled the backyard for a third time. He wasn't usually the one to give speeches, and I was sure the family was teasing him as another set of murmurs started up.

Grinning, Ashan nodded his head to one side and then the other. "Okay, enough. Thank you for the encouragement but I do have something to say." He took a couple of paces forward and waved at me to join him. I wasn't sure what was going on, but went to his side.

Ashan looked around at everyone as he spoke again. "Some of you may know and others perhaps not, but you may have suspected." He took my hand in his and turned to me. "Jamie is my wife; we have been married for some time now and are about to have a baby."

My mouth fell open from shock as more murmurs came from all directions. "We know, we can see that," Luder shouted from the back somewhere and everyone burst out in laughter.

"Yes, yes, yes," Ashan said, "We can all see the bump, I know. But you didn't all know that we had been married, now did you?" There were many "no's" coming through this time. He pulled a sparkling diamond ring from his pocket and added it to the thin one I already wore. My heart leaped as I stared at it in utter amazement. It was beyond perfect.

Turning back to the family beaming, Ashan continued. "Also, I want to declare that I will ensure my family and all our allies will wreak havoc on anyone who dares touch Jamie again." The late afternoon sky filled with cheers. Ashan pulled me into his arms and kissed me tenderly.

The staff brought out the meals and we all sat back down. The women all wanted to look at my new ring and congratulations done the round before anyone started eating. The food was brilliant, and we received many compliments. After supper, we all shared a round of cocktails before the family started heading home.

By the time everyone including the caterers and cleaners, left, it was just after nine. I made us some hot chocolate with mini marshmallows, and we sat outside watching the sky light up with stars. We sat next to each other on the wooden swing seat Luder had given us as a housewarming gift.

Ashan had them set it up between the patio and the jacuzzi. The air smelled of the ocean and we could hear the waves crashing on the shore. The evening was picture-perfect. Ashan took my hand and kissed my fingers as he turned to face me.

"Jamie," he said softly. Turning to him, Ashan held my thighs where the dress had fallen away, exposing them. "I love you," he breathed out. Leaning forward, I took his strong face in my hands. "Ashan, I love you too," I whispered, feeling tears form in my eyes.

He pulled me closer and kissed me passionately. Pulling back for air, I placed my hands on his muscular chest. Glancing down, I continued to speak. "I have something else to say as well."

Ashan lifted my head and gazed into my eyes. "Yes, hun?" he asked.

Grinning, I gave him the news. "We're having a girl."

Watching him, his face light up and his being shone brighter than the stars were the headline of my day. He stood and picked me up. "This calls for a celebration," he said as he carried me towards the jacuzzi room, but he didn't enter it.

My breath was blown away as he walked around the side and through a hidden archway. The archway was overgrown with vines, and no one would ever find it without knowing it was there.

Around the upper edges hung fairy lights, and down between the vines. The floor was covered in the most amazing flowers. It smelled of vanilla and honey and my senses lit up like the night sky. I felt like we had entered another world as Ashan moved slowly through it, turning in small circles.

Moving towards the side, I saw a bench covered by leaves. The base was lined with tender pink and purple flowers. Ashan placed me gently down and sat down beside me. "I found this a bit earlier this afternoon and thought you would like it." He whispered in my ear as he came closer and kissed my neck.

His lips were soft and his breath warm as it collided with the cool evening air, sending shivers down my spine. "It is truly beyond belief; I have never seen a place so magical," I whispered back as I got onto his lap pulling the front half of the dress up. Ashan slid his hand under the hanging back piece and firmly took hold of my butt, pulling me into him.

Pushing my hands up the nape of his neck and into his hair, out lips met with uncontrollable passion. Our kiss was hard, and I felt his dick coming to life under me as he squeezed my arse tighter. It was pumping in his pants begging to be released. I slid my hands down his shoulders and unbuttoned his shirt before moving down.

Shifting myself slightly back, I loosened his belt and unzipped his pants. The throbs were now quicker, and his dick was rock hard as I pulled it free from his underwear. Ashan breathed out heavily as I touched him.

"Oh, hun, I love you," he stated as he altered his position a tad bit on the bend to balance me on top of him. With his hands now free, he pulled the broad straps of the dress from my arms, lifting each through the sleeve to pull the dress's bodice down.

The cool air touched my skin and slid over my breasts, bringing my nipples to life. Ashan quickly came in for the rescue sucking first at one and then the other. Lifting my head, I allowed my moans to meet the night sky. Sucking and nibbling in turns at my nipples made me squirm a little.

His hands found their way through the tangle of dress now around my waist as I felt him pulling at my sheer mech linen thong. I heard it tear before I could budge so he could pull it down. With nothing between us now, Ashan lifted me a little and lowered me onto his pounding dick.

Gasping for air, I felt him filling me. His dick felt harder and larger than usual, but I welcomed it as lust filled every bone and muscle of my body. Flinging my head forward, I softly bit him in the neck and nibbled at his ear. Ashan held my ass firmly as he moved me up and down his shaft.

He moved slowly and then pumped me hard and fast a couple of times before slowing down again. After a couple of times, I felt like I was floating on clouds of desire. I leaned back ever so slightly and placed my hands on his knees so I could spread my legs wider, wanting more of him inside of me.

Closing my eyes and allowing my head to fall back between my shoulder blades, I breathed out sharply. Ashan brought his head in and nibbled at my nipples again, sending sparks through every inch of my body. I felt his hands move from my ass over my hips. Holding my hips with his fingertips, I felt his thumbs moving to my clitoris.

Using his thumbs, Ashan made slow circular movements, first with one and then the other thumb over my clitoris. I screamed into the night air as my body started to shake then he stopped pulling his thumbs away. Grabbing hold of my hips tightly, he moved me slowly up and down his shaft again.

I dug my nails into his legs as my body craved more. Stopping again, he moved his thumbs back to play with my clitoris again. Every inch of me trembled as I floated higher on ecstasy. Ashan pulled back again and took hold of my hips. This time, I flung up and grabbed him around the neck. "Fuck me, baby, please, make me cum," I breathed out. He was driving me crazy, and I was ready to explode onto him.

Feeling his hands moving back to my rear end, I was ready for him. Ashan lifted me up and down his dick in quick consecutive moves, but it didn't take a lot. By the third time he brought me down hard filling me, I cried out in pleasure as I came. He also came with me, roaring like a lion.

He held me for a while before carrying me back inside. I filled the tub with bubbles as Ashan made us some hot cocoa. After a long, soothing bath, we crawled into bed cuddling.

Over the next two weeks, we consulted the doctor on home birthing. After weighing all our options, we decided it was the way we wanted to go. It placed less stress on the mother and the child, and the doctor agreed to assist us.

We set up a small portable pool in Catalina's room so she would already be where she needed to be. With my last scan a week before my due date, the doctor informed us that the pregnancy went well, and he couldn't see any complications. Ashan also hired a home nurse who came to stay with us.

She would assist with the birth and the first week after Catalina came. I was initially nervous but settled with the idea as I counted off the days.

A sharp pain in my abdomen woke me. Looking out the window, I noticed it was still dark out. Moving carefully, I got up and went to the bathroom. My bladder felt like it was about to explode if I didn't. After using the toilet, I felt better, the pain was almost gone, and it was more like a dull throb than pain.

I got back into bed but couldn't fall asleep again, so I decided to get up. I didn't want to wake Ashan yet as I wasn't sure if it was time. Going downstairs, I poured a glass of juice and sat on the patio for a bit, admiring the stars and listening to the ocean.

After a while, I stood to go back inside. As I walked, I felt the dull throb becoming more prominent. Entering the kitchen, I knew that it was time. Ashan had installed a baby system as he called it. There was a button in each room of the house that rang on his phone when pressed.

It was for just such an occasion as this. Moving around the breakfast island, I found the button and pressed it. It was only seconds before Ashan appeared in the doorway.

"You rang," he said, sounding excited. "Is it time?"

Breathing slowly and deeply, I nodded my head. He came to my side and held me around the waist as we walked back upstairs. The nurse slept in Catalina's room on a spare bed we had brought in. She woke as soon as Ashan switched on the light.

"It's time," Ashan proclaimed as she rose.

Nodding, she called the doctor to let him know. Ashan walked with me up and down the hallway as ordered while she filled the pool with water and collected the towels and instruments the doctor had sent over the previous week. Standing in the doorway of Catalina's room she kept an eye on us.

As we passed her for what felt like the hundredth time, I had to stop and ask. "How long before the doctor comes?"

My breathing was slightly labored and the cramps sharper. "It's not a quick process. It can take all day, try to relax. Let me know when you feel a cramp so we can time them." She replied.

Nodding, we started walking again. Every time I felt a cramp, we stopped, and she timed the duration. She also kept note of how far apart each one was. They were still irregular and far apart. She brought out a large ball and had me sit on it, rolling in circles. "This will assist with the opening of the bones," she said.

It was well after breakfast and almost lunchtime when she called the doctor again. After speaking to him, she asked us to sit in the water for a bit until he came. Ashan sat behind me in his shorts as we did my breathing exercises together.

The doctor arrived about half an hour later and had me lie down so he could see how far I had dilated. "Well, well," he said smiling. "It's almost time."

We got back into the small pool and proceeded with more breathing techniques. Shortly after supper, Catalina was born. I held her to my chest overwhelmed by the reality and beauty of it all. She was perfect with tiny little hands and feet, and dark hair. I had never seen anything as precious as her.

Kissing her head softly, I whispered through my crying. "Welcome to the world, Catalina."

Ashan was leaning around me, caressing her tiny little arm. Glancing at him, I noticed he was also crying out of joy. She was a healthy weight and had the lungs of an elephant. After the nurse cleaned her and the doctor checked her out, the nurse gave me instructions on feeding her. She sat with me to make sure I came right.

Ashan had left to see the doctor out and grab something to eat. He brought some supper for us as well. I couldn't believe how hungry I was. He held Catalina against his bare chest as I ate softly, humming to her. I knew he was going to be a great father, and this proved it.

The first week wasn't as bad as I had imagined. Once the nurse left, things got a bit harder, but the joy outweighed the troubles. Ashan arranged a naming gathering for the entire family to come to meet our little angel. During the next couple of weeks, he handled everything.

He was hands-on with diaper changes, and baths. He even did most of the cooking for us. I couldn't have asked for a better man and was genuinely astounded at all he did.

Time appeared to be flying past us as days turned to weeks, and weeks to months. Before we knew it our little angel was turning one. She had taken her first stepps, had four teeth and were chatting away in a language of her own.

Ashan now ran three gambling dens and were working on acquiring more. Our days were getting fuller and fuller but we couldn't complain. Sometimes trouble knocked at the door sure, but nothing as tough as what we had lived through.

Epilogue - Ashan

"Catalina, slow down,"

"Jamie, let her run, she's just a little girl," I said, squeezing Jamie's hand as we entered the third Gambling Den out of the six, we now own. "She's safe here; the staff loves her, and she knows our routine by now."

"Yes, Ashan, I know but she can still get herself into trouble, don't you think?" Jamie replied, grinning up at me. "We love coming with you once a week to the den and checking in on your success," she added raising to her toes as she kissed me on the cheek. "But she needs to stay close so I can make sure she doesn't cause any trouble as little ones tend to do. You know." She turned her head and lifted her eyes for the last part, making me smile.

Jamie was still as beautiful as the day we got married, and with each passing year, my love for her seemed to grow. The last couple of days she appeared to have a glow about her. I couldn't put my finger on it, but felt sure something was up. She hadn't spoken about it, and I would wait until she was ready, but I felt sure she may be pregnant again.

Pulling her into my arms, I kissed her hard. "You know I love you so much," I breathed out letting go.

"I know," Jamie responded as she turned and headed after Catalina. I stood watching as the two entered the restaurant area before heading up to my office. Once I checked all my mail and ensured operations were running smoothly, I looked for them.

As expected, I found them in the kitchen. Catalina was sitting on one of the counters, and Jamie was standing beside her, holding her. The head chef was making them milkshakes as usual. I stood in the door for a bit, admiring my girls. Catalina's dark locks hung over her shoulders, framing her pretty face.

Most people who meet us together always comment on how much she looks just like me. But I see Jamie in her smile, her laughter, and her attitude. After receiving their milkshakes, they head out the back door to the little picnic spot I set up last year for the workers. The two sat basking in the sun, enjoying their drinks filling my heart with love.

I waited a while so they could at least finish their drinks before stepping out. "Come on girls, we still have a couple left to do," I said, waving at them.

Catalina jumped right up and trotted over, grabbing my leg and hanging on to it. "Daddy, Daddy, we had milk." She said, smiling widely at me.

Patting her head, I replied softly. "Yes, I saw honey, what flavor did you have?"

With a twinkle in her eyes, she replied loudly, almost screaming at me. "Strawberry like always."

Glancing at Jamie, with a smile, I continued. "Now we have to go. Are you ready?"

Catalina let go of my leg and ran to the door screaming over her shoulder. "Come, Mommy, come."

Jamie was already at my side, and we headed back in. Once they gave their glasses to the washer, we left and went to the next den. On our way there, Jamie received a call from Evelina. She nodded as she spoke and agreed.

She turned to me as she hung up. "Something has come up that they are going to need my help with. Can you drop me at Leo's house?" Jamie said.

"Don't you have a class this afternoon teaching those brilliant young minds all about computers?" I replied.

Jamie smiled, "Yes, I do, and I'll be done in time. They just need to stop an attack on Luder's system and need to find out who is trying to invade him."

Shaking my head, I turned up to the next street and traveled to Leo's place. "So, should I pick you up in a bit, or will Leo drop you off, then I can get you afterward?" I inquired as we pulled up to his gate.

Jamie gave me a quick kiss on the cheek as she got out. "I'll have Leo drop me for the class and you can pick me up." Glancing at Catalina, she continued. "I love you both, be a good girl and listen to Daddy, okay." Jamie sent her a kiss and closed the door.

Catalina shook her head and waved at Jamie as she went inside. I drove off once she was inside and headed to the other three dens. Cleo was the manager at the one and she kept an eye on Catalina while I did my checks.

At the second last den, Catalina walked with me. But I had to carry her for the last bit when her legs got tired. Frank sat with her in my office at the last den, looking at dog videos on my computer.

After making sure everything was running according to procedure, I took Catalina to her dancing lesson. She was doing well but wasn't a top dancer. Yet, she enjoyed it so how good she was didn't matter. Life was about having fun.

Leo called as I waited for Catalina. "Hey, how's things going?" I asked, answering my phone.

"Great man, Jamie caught the guy trying to access Luder's network and secured it again. I dropped her off for class, just wanted to let you know." Leo said.

"Thanks, Leo, I'll get her once Catalina's dance class is done. Have a good one."

"A good evening to you too," Leo added before hanging up.

Catalina's class was still half an hour. Once she was done, we grabbed some Chinese and headed to collect Jamie. Jamie's computer class had just finished when we arrived. I greeted her young students as they left the premises.

She offered classes twice a week for young adults who wanted to learn more about working with and on computers. The technology era created a great need for learning, and Jamie knew a lot. She was proud that she could provide greatly needed protective computing classes.

It was better to be safe than sorry, she always said. You didn't need to know how to hack if you knew how to prevent it. She was working the pro-active approach, and the students loved it.

Jamie was delighted by our selection of food for supper. As we headed home, she talked about her students and who she thought would make it big in the industry. She loved what she did and always talked about it passionately. I thought our lives couldn't get any better, but then Jamie ended the conversation with something that made me wonder.

"The family is gathering tomorrow evening at Roman's place and Evelina said we have to be there on time." Jamie smiled at me, winking as she spoke.

"What, what do you mean, we're always on time, and why didn't Leo mention it when I spoke to him?" I replied as we entered our mansion. "What's going on, why do I get the feeling you're hiding something?"

Jamie walked to the kitchen, ignoring my questions and I knew they were planning something. Knowing Jamie, there was no way she would give up details, I would just have to wait. Jamie took Catalina upstairs for her bath after supper while I caught up on some work before bedtime.

She was tucking Catalina in as I entered our child's room. "Time for a story?" I inquired rolling my eyes at Catalina. She giggled and shook her head wildly. "Right, if you're all settled, I'll start."

Jamie kissed my forehead as she left, and I sat on the edge of the bed. I was halfway through my made-up story of a princess who lost her dancing abilities when I noticed Catalina was fast asleep. Ensuring she was nicely covered, I kissed her gently on the head before leaving.

I found Jamie in the tub, and it was filled with bubbles. "So, now you're bathing alone?" I asked, raising my eyebrows at her.

"Oh, no, I would never dream of it," she replied, laughing. "I was just keeping it warm until you came. You see, I knew you would be done quickly."

Undressing, I responded. "Really, and how did you know that? She could have been awake for hours."

Getting into the bath behind Jamie as she moved forward, I was glad Catalina hadn't been awake any longer. I might have missed a session with Jamie.

"Well," she replied, laying back against my chest so I could lather her. "I saw after supper she was quite tired. Remember, I'm her mother, I know these things." Jamie grinned at me over her shoulder.

Giving in, we washed and headed to bed. I also felt drained from the day's activities; by the sound of it, tomorrow would be a long day.

JAMIE

I woke up early and prepared breakfast while Ashan was still sleeping. The family was throwing a surprise party tonight and I was too excited to sleep further. It was still dark out, but it gave me enough time to bake some croissants. Catalina loved them just as much as Ashan, and I wanted today to be perfect.

The sun was waking the world outside by the time they came out of the oven. I made a pot of coffee and prepared a tray with coffee, croissants, and juice for Catalina, and added some fresh diced fruit. Admiring my handy work, I was ready to wake them. Heading upstairs, I placed the tray on the side table by our bedroom door.

I first woke Catalina. After she was washed and dressed, we headed to wake Ashan. Entering the room, I collected the tray from the table. Ashan wasn't in bed as I expected. He was already up and getting dressed. "Good morning, my dears," he said, looking at us as we entered. "Wow, look at that," he stated as Catalina jumped onto the bed and hugged him.

Smiling at him, I leaned over and gave him a quick kiss. "Good morning hun," I added as he took the tray.

"This looks lovely, and there's enough for all of us," Ashan added beaming. "You must have been up half the night, thank you."

Catalina settled next to him and took a croissant from the tray as he placed it down between them. I joined them for breakfast on the bed and afterward, we got ready to head out.

The day went reasonably quickly as we kept busy, even the visits to the gambling dens went faster than usual. It was as if Ashan was rushing through the day to get to the afternoon. He seemed overly eager and excited. I was glad he looked forward to spending the afternoon with our family, as I did.

We arrived on time and most of the family were already present. Walking to the back where the gathering was to be held, I was in awe. It looked like something out of a fairytale. There was an arch set up by the entrance to the house filled with pink and blue balloons and ribbons.

The tables were also covered with either blue or pink tablecloths, and rainbow-colored teddies were on top in the middle. Some were in what looked like hot-air balloons, others were in little baskets, and then there were ones on rocking horses. The bar area was also covered in balloons, lint bows, and flowers. The place truly looked stunning.

"What's all of this, is someone having a baby, or did I forget one of the children's birthdays?" Ashan asked as he greeted Roman.

Roman glanced at me, raising his eyebrows. Ashan turned and looked at me, lowering my head, I felt sure the smile on my face was going to tear through it. Ashan went down on one knee to look into my eyes. "Yes, hun, we're pregnant," I whispered.

His face lit up like a New Year ball at midnight as he picked me up and turned in a circle. Placing me down, Ashan kissed me intensely. The family all cheered and came closer to congratulate us. As Ashan pulled back from our kiss, I noticed the glimmer of tears in his eyes. Turning to face the family, he lifted his hands in the air as he shouted. "We're having another baby."

With the news out in the open, we could start. After everyone hugged, kissed, and gave their congratulations, it was time for the men to visit one side by the pool. Karine had arranged for babysitters to keep the kids entertained while we proceeded with our planned schedule.

After a couple of silly games, it was time for the gifts. The men joined us for this as both Ashan, and I had to guess what was in the present and who it was from before we could open them. There was lots of clothing, in neutral colors, of course. Then there were blankies, towels, toys, and so much more.

We got most of the item guesses incorrect, but who they were from, we had most correct. At least we knew our family well it seemed, even if we didn't truly know their idea of gifts. Once the gifts were all opened and stored in the car, we could sit down for supper. It was a good afternoon and evening.

Back home, Ashan and I started planning the nursery. The next couple of months were going to be tiring as we turned the nursery we had into a room for Catalina.

We contacted the same contractors who assisted the first time as their work was exceptional. It took us a couple of weeks to make a final decision, but once we did, we could move ahead.

Over the course of a couple of months, we got everything in place. We moved the study down a floor to make room for the nursery and couldn't wait for the new addition to our family to arrive. Life couldn't be better.

THE END

ABOUT LEXI ASHER

Lexi Asher gave up a promising career in the medical field to focus entirely on her family—and her writing. She lives in the beautiful, luscious Virginia countryside with her husband, 3 young children and 4 pets.

The Ashers' rustic cottage is bustling with activity all day long, so when Lexi wants to get her head down and let her creative juices flow, she will often take refuge in their beautifully ornate conservatory where Lexi does most of her writing.

When it comes to love, Lexi is a big believer in second chances—sometimes you just meet the right person at the wrong time. So, her stories often feature old flames that are reignited and broken hearts that are mended. But is love really better the second time around? Well, read and find out!

BOOKS BY LEXI ASHER

"Morozov Bratva" Series

The Russian Bratva of Miami has three rules: solve problems with violence, paint the streets with blood, and break hearts at will. They're not nice, they're not gentle, and they don't compromise. But behind closed doors, they'll show you what ruthless love really means.

Kidnapped by the Bratva

A Secret Baby by the Bratva

Pregnant by the Bratva

Sold to the Bratva

Forbidden by the Bratva

Surrogate for the Bratva

Bullied by the Bratva

Betrayed by the Bratva

Auctioned to the Bratva

Hostage of the Bride

Used by the Bratva

"Small Town Billionaires" Series

Pretend for the Billionaire

The Billionaire's Baby

"The Crenshaw Billionaire Brothers" Series

Billionaire Brothers is where grumpiness and pain give way to romance and love. These loaded heirs may seem to have it all: money to burn, looks to die for, women to spoil. But it takes a special someone, a magical spark to reveal the real man behind the facade.

Grumpy Billionaire

Bossy Billionaire

Daddy Billionaire

"Lakeside Love" Series

Riverroad is a small town where everyone knows everyone, where the guy you've known since childhood turns into the hottest hunk around, where friends become lovers, and where everyday interactions between neighbors might just turn into steamy encounters when you least expect it...

Chasing A Second Chance

Chasing The Doctor Next Door

Chasing A Fake Wedding

Chasing The Cowboy

Printed in Dunstable, United Kingdom